DANCE WITH ME

Line dance instructor Lisa Gates desperately needs a new venue, and has her heart set on the Cliff Hotel. The new owner, shrewd business-man Ken Huntley, has plans to revamp the building, and is adamant Lisa's classes won't fit its elite new image. However, in an amazing about turn, he agrees to accommo-date her for a brief period preceding the refurbishment — on the proviso that he works alongside her as her DJ. What can she do but agree . . . ?

JANET CHAMBERLAIN

DANCE WITH ME

Complete and Unabridged

LINFORD
Leicester

First published in Great Britain in 2006

First Linford Edition
published 2007

British Library CIP Data

Chamberlain, Janet
    Dance with me.—Large print ed.—
Linford romance library
1. Love stories
2. Large type books
I. Title
823.9′2 [F]

ISBN 978–1–84617–871–9

Published by
F. A. Thorpe (Publishing)
Anstey, Leicestershire

Set by Words & Graphics Ltd.
Anstey, Leicestershire
Printed and bound in Great Britain by
T. J. International Ltd., Padstow, Cornwall

This book is printed on acid-free paper

'My Future Is In Ruins!'

Ken Huntley stared in surprise at the strange vision in front of him. In her cowboy boots, fringed shirt, suede skirt and Stetson, this young woman wouldn't have looked out of place on the set of 'Oklahoma'. But what was she doing here, at the Cliff Hotel? And why was she staring at him with such blatant anger in her startling blue eyes?

She had to be an actress, he decided. No one else would barge into his office decked out in such an outfit. Unless, of course, it was a wind-up. Any minute now, that harsh expression would melt into amusement and she'd reveal herself as a novelty kissogram . . . wouldn't she?

'If you'd like to leave your gun-belt outside and take a seat, maybe we can sort out . . . '

'This isn't a joking matter,' she cut

in, ignoring his offer and remaining standing. 'You're the new owner of this hotel, I take it?'

'That's right.'

'Well, because of you, my whole future is in ruins!'

'I think this must be a case of mistaken identity,' Ken told her pleasantly. 'I don't believe I've had the pleasure of ever meeting you, let alone ruining your future, Miss . . . ?'

'Lisa Gates. The line dance instructor,' she added as though it explained everything. Well, it explained the get-up, at least.

He allowed himself a slightly more leisurely survey of Miss Lisa Gates, taking in the dark tumble of curls spiralling in soft disarray over the shoulders of her fringed white shirt, and the way her skimpy splash of a mini-skirt accentuated every curve of her long, booted legs.

'I'm Ken Huntley,' he supplied, being careful not to smile. 'But I imagine you already know that.' He eased himself back into his chair. 'Now, perhaps you'd like to explain how I've inadvertently ruined your future? Then, if it's within my power, I'll do my best to make amends.'

'It *is* within your power,' Lisa Gates assured him, a flicker of hope animating her clear features. 'All you need to do is reinstate my classes.'

She'd lost him again.

Her frown re-appeared as she explained: 'At six o'clock this evening, I had a phone call from the organisation that arranges my bookings.' She paused and looked searchingly into his face.

He gave an encouraging nod. 'I'm not with you yet, but go on.'

'They told me that my line dance classes wouldn't be transferring to the Cliff Hotel after all.'

Ken had a vague recollection. 'Yes, I did cancel some dance classes, but that was over a month ago. Surely you haven't only just found out?'

'*When* I found out isn't the issue here. What I want to know is *why.*'

He rubbed a hand over his jaw as he tried to recall the details. Cancelling a handful of dance classes with an out-of-town organisation had seemed a reasonably simple task at the time. Of course, he'd had no way of knowing then that it would lead to a run-in with some feisty, long-legged slip of a girl with a penchant for fancy dress.

He studied the obstinate set of her mouth and felt a flicker of regret that she hadn't turned out to be a kissogram girl after all.

'And if I tell you why, you'll go away and leave me in peace?'

'Not until you reinstate my classes.'

It was a pity she had such a brusque manner, he reflected. She was quite something with her flawless complexion and vibrant blue eyes. Something about the way the whole package was put together had elevated her out of the ordinary.

'Well?' she demanded.

He tossed down his pen and stood up. 'I'm sorry, but I can't do that.'

An uneasy silence stretched between them.

Lisa broke it. 'You've got to,' she whispered, desperation lacing her every word. 'I've not only told my students that we'll be moving here at the start of next month . . . I've had leaflets printed, booked newspaper advertisements . . . ' Her voice cracked slightly. 'I've even taken out a loan to buy a more powerful sound system.'

Ken felt for the girl, he really did, but he was running a business, and he was too experienced a manager to let sentiment cloud the issue.

'Look, I'm truly sorry,' he went on, hoping a calm, concerned manner would go some way towards diffusing the tension, 'but as I explained to your organisation, there have been quite a few changes at this hotel in the weeks since I took it over.'

'And?'

'Unfortunately, your classes are one of the casualties.'

'But I had an agreement — '

'It was my father, not me, who agreed to introduce line dancing into the hotel's agenda, and he wasn't in the best of health at the time.'

'So you're saying what? That he didn't know what he was doing?'

He was trying to be tactful but she wasn't making it very easy for him.

'I'm saying that maybe he wasn't as astute in his dealings as he should have been. Since his death, I've discovered a number of other unfortunate decisions, all of which I — '

Her expression shifted to outrage. 'How can you label my classes an unfortunate decision when they've proved a phenomenal success? People are flocking to the pier in their dozens.'

'In which case, why not continue working from there?'

She sighed impatiently. 'Haven't you heard? The place has been sold.'

'And that makes a difference?'

'Of course it does! It's been bought by a chain of nightclub owners and they want me out in a couple of weeks.'

'I don't wish to sound unsympathetic but is there any reason why you couldn't set your sights a bit lower and operate from, say, a church hall?'

She gave a snort of disbelief. 'I'm set to expand my business into a full-time career — I can't do that from a church hall.'

Ken frowned. Surely there were other places she could use? Sandford was a thriving seaside resort; his wasn't the only hotel in town.

He searched in his mind for a solution. 'I really can't offer you the Cliff Hotel, but as a gesture of goodwill, I'll put out a few feelers and see if I can find you similar premises.'

'There are no similar premises,' she countered. 'I need a large room with a bar, a stage, and a maple-sprung floor. Your ballroom is the only other place in the whole resort that matches my requirements.'

Ken heaved a weary sigh. 'Look, can we forget about your requirements for a moment and focus some attention on mine?'

Her eyes searched his face. 'What do you mean?'

'Over the coming months I'm planning to refurbish the entire building.' He spoke slowly, choosing his words with care. 'And in anticipation of that, I'm only retaining bookings for those functions which I feel are in keeping with the hotel's new image.'

A flush of crimson touched Lisa's cheeks. 'Oh, I get it — you're saying that my classes are too tacky for the likes of your snooty new hotel and you don't want them lowering the tone.'

He smiled at her description. 'You're putting words into my mouth.'

'But that's what you're thinking, isn't it?' She took a triumphant step towards him and the warm cinnamon scent of her perfume wafted over him, causing him to lose concentration for a moment.

★   ★   ★

'I prefer not to go down that route,' he managed at last. 'Let's just say that your classes aren't suitable and leave it at that.'

'It's a pity you're not more like your father,' she blurted out. 'He had both vision and trust, but I guess they're not qualities that are inherited.'

For some reason the comparison stung. Then Ken remembered who he was dealing with — an idealistic young woman, who had no experience of the stark realities of the business world.

'Miss Gates, my father was a wonderful man in many ways, but he had a tendency to put sentiment before business — a mistake I'm not about to make.'

Lisa drew herself up to her full height. 'I doubt he was as naïve as you think. William Huntley was well-respected in this town, and you don't achieve that by being a soft touch.'

Ken threw her an impatient look. Keen as he was to be rid of Lisa Gates, he didn't want her going away with the impression that his father's knack of collecting lame ducks in any way constituted good business.

'If not naïve, then he was certainly misguided on occasions.' He gestured towards the tall sash window. 'If you take a look across the car park, you'll see a dilapidated old Twenties theatre, bought by my father some years ago. Not to convert or develop, I might add — simply to provide an authentic meeting place for himself and a handful of old film buffs, to watch their collection of vintage reels.'

Lisa stalked over to the window and stared out. 'That's amazing,' she breathed, as if speaking to herself.

'From what I gather, nobody ever paid any admission and he even supplied the popcorn for nothing!'

'So where's the crime in that?' she said, turning to face him. 'Old buildings should be conserved as part of the town's heritage. It's wonderful that he didn't knock it down.'

He shook his head in disbelief.

'Knocking it down would have been the best option for that old eyesore. He could have built a smart new car park on the site and extended the hotel over the old one.'

'That's what you're planning to do, isn't it?' She rolled her eyes heavenward. 'Of course! Anything with the least bit of novelty or character has no place in your slick modern schemes.'

His patience was fast running out. 'If by that you mean hordes of middle-aged women decked out in frilly doilies, then no, there's definitely no place for them in my hotel.'

Her eyes glittered, but her voice remained calm. Dangerously so. 'You're good at making assumptions aren't you, Mr Huntley? You won't believe me if I tell you that there's nothing frilly or middle-aged about my dancers, so why don't you come and see for yourself?'

Ken was taken aback when her face was suddenly transformed by a wide smile which dimpled her cheeks and showed perfect white teeth.

'Come on — don't be a stick-in-the-mud. You might even enjoy it.'

'Miss Gates, I really don't think — ' he began.

'I'm on my way to class now.' There was a sudden vibrancy in her manner and her voice was filled with enthusiasm. 'But if you can't make that, there's another on Tuesday night and again on Thursday afternoon.'

Would she never give up?

'I'm sorry, that's not possible. I've . . . a stack of paperwork to get through. So, if you'll excuse me, I'd like to press on.'

'Don't worry,' she said, in a confidential tone. 'I've lots to get on with as well. First I need to prepare some details for my solicitor.'

Again there was that brilliant smile, but this time it unnerved him. She smoothed her skirt over her shapely hips and walked towards the door.

'You know,' she added in a matter-of-fact tone, 'when people begin to realise what a cold, unfeeling person now owns the Cliff Hotel, they might not be so impressed by its sparkling new image.'

So that was her game!

'You should get out more,' she added as a parting shot. 'What sort of man spends his Friday evenings shut away in a dusty old office?'

He didn't answer.

'Don't forget, Tuesday and Thursdays,' she said. 'It would do you good to get away from . . . all the paperwork.' Her glance at his empty desk was pointed. 'See you at my classes,' she called out as she left.

'Not on your life,' he muttered, shaking his head to rid himself of the image of those captivating eyes and long slender legs.

* * *

Well, she'd done it now! She'd be lucky if Mr Stuffed Shirt ever let her within fifty feet of the Cliff Hotel in future. Now all she had to do was figure out how she could possibly afford a solicitor.

Could Philip's father be persuaded to help out, she wondered, reaching her car. Senior partner in a large firm of solicitors, he'd certainly be a match for Ken Huntley. But would it be in order to ask him?

It was one thing asking a favour from your boyfriend, but expecting cheap advice from a possible future father-in-law was totally different.

She started the engine. It caught for a moment and then died. She tried again . . . nothing! Oh no! Thanks to that insufferable man, she was already running late for her class and now it looked as if she wouldn't make it at all.

With a snarl, she retraced her steps back to the hotel to phone a taxi.

'Sorry.' The reply was the same from every taxi firm she tried. 'We can't send a car right now. Friday night's one of our busiest times.'

There was nothing for it but to go back to her car and wait.

Meanwhile, Ken sighed. Despite his relief at having got rid of her, Lisa Gates' visit had provided one of the more interesting interludes since he'd taken over the hotel. But now he had to get back to work.

Picking up yet another bulging file, he gave a frustrated groan. All this stuff should be on computer in this day and age. It was soul destroying having to wade through endless sheets of paper, and so typical of his father to have retained such an antiquated system.

Soul destroying, but also very necessary, he reminded himself. All kinds of problems could be buried in those piles of papers and the only way to find out was to read through each and every one.

But as he checked, double-checked and cross-referenced, one niggling question kept rising to the forefront of his mind. What if Calamity Jane was right about him being a stick-in-the-mud? Was it possible that he had lost his spontaneity somewhere along the way and all these extra hours in the office were turning him into a sad workaholic?

He couldn't remember when he'd last taken a day off. Perhaps he should take her advice and put the paperwork on hold.

★ ★ ★

Growing more and more agitated with each passing minute, Lisa rested her forehead on the steering wheel and squeezed her eyes shut. This really wasn't her night. Even ringing Philip wasn't an option. Three weeks ago she'd found herself stranded outside the pier, and he'd refused point blank to come out and collect her.

'I'm with some clients,' he'd told her when he'd finally answered her call. 'And walking out of the meeting to come and rescue you will turn out far more expensive than you phoning a taxi.'

He'd been right, of course. His

16

hourly rate as an accountant was far higher than the price of a taxi. But as she'd waited on the desolate, windswept promenade, she'd begun to wish he didn't have quite such an industrious attitude to work.

A knock on the window caused Lisa to jump. But as she turned to see who it was, her heart gave a lurch. Instead of the taxi driver she'd been hoping for, Ken Huntley was standing there.

She wound down the window.

'I thought you'd gone,' he said. 'Is there a problem?'

'My car won't start,' she said, 'so unless you have any objection, I'm going to wait here until my taxi arrives.'

He looked surprised. 'Why should I have any objection?' he asked.

She shrugged petulantly. 'My wreck of a car might lower the tone of your car park.'

'You really don't have a very high opinion of me, do you?' He crouched to bring his face on a level with hers. 'Believe it or not I came over to see if I could help,' he said gently.

The scent of his aftershave drifted through the open window, stirring her senses and throwing her emotions into a spin. She closed her eyes and inhaled. It was warm earth and summer rainstorms and woods in autumn. It was cedar and fir cones. It was masculine and unique and . . .

Perturbed by the direction her thoughts were taking, she fixed him with a cold stare. 'It's all taken care of. My taxi will be here any minute.'

He gave her a doubtful look. 'Want to bet on it? Friday's one of their busiest evenings; you'd be better off catching a bus.'

'With my sound system and CDs? I don't think so.'

'Well, can I give you a lift, then?'

Lisa stared back at him. She had a class to get to and alternatives weren't exactly coming thick and fast.

'Shouldn't you be doing something a little higher on your list of priorities — like sifting through a pile of paperwork?'

He gave a sudden wide grin. 'Nope. I've decided to call it a day.'

'I see. Well, I suppose it would be a help,' she conceded, determined not to appear too eager. 'Although I can't imagine why you're suddenly being so nice to me.'

His expression turned rueful. 'Maybe to prove that I'm not the cold, hard-hearted businessman you seem to have me marked down as.'

So he did have some humane qualities after all! She pulled the key from the ignition. 'You don't have to do this.'

'I know. But I want to.' The warmth in his voice was unexpected.

'I — ' She drew a deep breath.

'I take it that's a yes then?' he said, the smile back on his face. 'Now, come on — let's get your gear loaded into my car.'

'But — the taxi,' she faltered. 'I've already phoned . . . '

He gave an exaggerated sigh. 'I'll ring and cancel it on my mobile. Now, are you coming or not?'

What choice did she have? By the time the taxi finally showed up, all her students could have tired of waiting and gone home.

⋆　⋆　⋆

When he pulled up outside the pier, Ken realised that Lisa hadn't been exaggerating about her classes being well attended. A sizeable crowd had collected around the entrance and the queue stretched quite a long way along the promenade — and not a frilly doily in sight, he noted with surprise, his eyes taking in a prominent group of young people, all wearing fashionable clothes.

'The first priority is to get everyone inside,' she told him as they began to unload. She threw him a tentative smile. 'Any chance you could carry this gear to the stage while I take the money at the door?'

He could do better than that, he decided, picking up the sound system and following Lisa along the wooden decking to the pavilion. He'd spent part of his student days working on a mobile disco and was more than capable of connecting up a few leads.

He found a sturdy trestle table at the back of the stage and, relying heavily on guesswork, carried it to the front, draped it with the voluminous American flag he'd found folded in Lisa's case of CDs and set everything up on top of it. Right — he could go! The idea was vaguely disappointing — which was stupid. He had better things to do than hang around a dilapidated old pier.

He bent to pick up his jacket. It was then that he noticed a cardboard box containing plastic cups and a huge bottle of orange squash.

He glanced towards the entrance. A steady stream of customers showed no sign of letting up. Lisa would be hard pressed to mix up the drinks, he decided, giving himself the excuse he needed.

He picked up the box and headed in the direction of a small serving hatch.

He wasn't above mixing up a few litres of orange squash.

When the flow of dancers eased a little, Lisa tucked her cashbox away, put on her headset microphone, and began to welcome everybody.

Only ten minutes late, she thought with relief, thanks to Ken Huntley stepping in to help. But if he thought he was off the hook now, he'd clearly underestimated her. She'd have told him so too, if he'd hung around. But after setting up, he had disappeared.

Not that she was sorry. He might have the type of looks that fuelled fantasies, but the rest of him just didn't match up. His eagerness to discard the old for the new was callous in the extreme. She just felt sorry for his wife or girlfriend.

Now where had that thought come from? she muttered to herself, as she adjusted her microphone. She couldn't care two hoots about him — or his significant other — and she was glad he hadn't hung around.

A Surprise For Lisa

On the other side of the hatch, Ken had finished pouring out the juice when he heard Lisa welcoming her students, and he couldn't resist opening the hatch just a fraction to see if she looked as friendly and inviting as she sounded. The fiery little tornado who'd stormed into his office clearly had a softer side to her, there was no question about it. From the brightness of her smile to the set of her delectably feminine body, she radiated an aura of warmth and humour and vitality.

It struck him that somehow, standing up on the stage in the spotlight's harsh glare, she seemed far more vulnerable than she had before.

Don't go getting all protective over her, he told himself sternly. There was no place for Miss Lisa Gates at the Cliff

Hotel. Once the refurbishments were finished, this young woman in her cowboy get-up would be totally at odds with the place.

It was a pity, though, he thought. There was something about her that made him long to get to know her better.

★ ★ ★

Lisa had taken her class through three or four dances when a movement from behind the hatch made her uneasy. Someone was watching her from the kitchen!

'Here's a dance you should all know.' Heart pounding, she put on some traditional country music. 'See how you go with 'Ribbon Of Highway'. I'm just going to take a minute to get my breath back.'

It was probably just one of the dancers taking a break from the crowd, she assured herself, as she jumped down from the stage. On the other hand, what if it was some low-life after the takings?

But as she cautiously approached, the doors slowly swung open to reveal a smiling Ken Huntley. 'Much as I'm enjoying our little game of Peek-a-Boo,' he told her, 'I need a quick word.'

'What are you still doing here? I thought you'd left ages ago.'

He gestured towards a table, where several dozen plastic cups had been neatly lined up in rows. 'I thought you could do with some help with the refreshments.'

'Oh . . . I'd forgotten about the drinks,' she said, feeling foolish. 'Thanks. That's saved my skin.'

She paused to study him. He looked different. He'd discarded his jacket and tie, and with the neck of his shirt undone and the sleeves rolled up, he looked nothing like the hardened businessman who'd been so obstructive back in his office.

Was Ken Huntley actually enjoying himself enough to let go of his arrogant, managerial image?

He grinned, which just reinforced the idea. 'Glad to be of service. Now, would you like me to line them up on the counter?'

'They'll be fine where they are for the moment,' she answered, aware that their conversation was beginning to attract attention. 'Thank you,' she murmured again, lowering her eyes to the table. Suddenly, for no discernible reason, she felt as awkward as a teenager. 'And thanks for the lift too. But please don't let me keep you any longer.'

To her surprise he made no move to leave but instead leaned nonchalantly against the counter and began moving in time to the music.

'Don't tell me you're trying to get rid of me,' he teased, inclining his head so he didn't have to shout over the music. 'I'm just starting to get into the swing of things.'

Lisa's eyes widened in surprise. 'But I didn't think you . . . '

A wicked glint sparkled in his eyes. 'Even a stick-in-the-mud needs some time off,' he told her, prompting a flood of heat to her face as she recalled her earlier jibe. 'I think this is as good a time as any, don't you?'

'Well, certainly if — '

'Especially since I received a personal invitation,' he continued, cutting her off in mid-sentence. 'And do you know something? I'm enjoying every minute of it.' A smile curved the corners of his mouth.

She didn't believe him for a moment. But as the music came to an end and people began to drift off the floor, she couldn't waste any more time trying to figure out what his game was.

He was laughing at her! That much was obvious. But if there was the slightest chance he might be persuaded to reconsider his decision, she'd be crazy to send him away.

★　★　★

'Everybody on the floor! Get those hips moving!'

Her stage presence was amazing, Ken reflected as he continued to observe the class, this time from a seat at a table. Her students obviously thought so too, for they hung on her every word, responding with foot stomping, thigh slapping enthusiasm.

'It's a wonder they can't hear you in Tokyo,' he remarked to one young enthusiast, who'd taken time out from the class to cool down.

The young man gave a grin. 'Yeah, we're lucky there are no neighbours to make a fuss. When Lisa first started out, she hired a room above a restaurant and the owner had so many complaints about the noise, he told her we either had to wear soft shoes or sling our hooks.'

The sudden vision of leggy Lisa leading her class in a pair of fluffy pink carpet slippers caused Ken to laugh out loud.

He couldn't have timed it more

badly. At the precise moment the music faded, his laughter reverberated across the silence.

He muttered an oath. He should go straight over to her and explain that he hadn't been laughing at her or her class, despite the way it must seem. But as he rose to his feet, her instruction to clear the floor had him sitting back down again.

His laughter hadn't escaped Lisa's notice. Clearly, this evening was one big joke to him and had been right from the start. Well, she'd had enough of him amusing himself at her expense. Let him take a turn at being in the spotlight, and see if he found that equally entertaining.

'The next dance is the County Line,' she announced. 'A classic cha-cha-cha. And as we have quite a few gentlemen with us tonight, some of you might like to try it as a partner dance. So if you could remain in your seats, I'll put the music on and demonstrate the sweetheart hold.'

Then, as the room fell quiet, she switched off her head-mike, jumped down from the stage and walked directly across to Ken.

'Would you mind?' she purred, extending her hand. 'I need someone to help me for a couple of minutes.'

She had only intended to have him demonstrate the hold and then, provided he looked suitably chastened, let him swiftly off the hook. But instead of the hesitant compliance she had anticipated, he jumped to his feet and took her outstretched hand with enthusiasm.

'I'm flattered you chose me,' he murmured as she positioned herself with her back against his chest.

'I thought you would be,' she lied, slightly flustered. She switched her head mike back on. 'Now just follow my instructions when the music starts and you won't have any problems.'

Well, maybe just one or two, hopefully. A smile flitted over her lips. She would leave him to flounder just enough to see what it felt like to be in the spotlight and vulnerable to wise-cracks. And after that, he'd be less likely to make fun of her, and might even take himself off home.

The dreamy ballad she'd chosen had a longer-than-average introduction, and as she waited for her cue to come in, she realised with some surprise that being cradled against Ken Huntley's warm, strong chest wasn't an altogether unpleasant sensation. In fact, she was so absorbed in figuring out how she could possibly enjoy being so close to somebody she didn't even like that she missed the start of the dance.

'Ah, at last,' he observed when she finally made a move. 'I was beginning to think you'd got so cosy that you'd fallen asleep.'

She stiffened and pulled away. But he continued to match his steps to hers with all the aplomb of a seasoned dancer. He was no more a beginner than she was! There was nothing for it, then but to keep her mind on the dance, and make sure he didn't realise how his closeness affected her.

That was easier said than done. Somehow he'd managed to pull her back tight against his chest, and the sensation of his warm body moving alongside hers was playing havoc with her running commentary. Every now and then she found herself stumbling over her instructions in a rather shaky voice. If she wasn't careful, she'd be the one who ended up looking foolish, while he emerged with his dignity intact.

It couldn't have ended soon enough for her, although some treacherous part of Lisa's brain, the part connected to her nerve endings, was wishing it could go on for ever.

'Music's over,' Ken murmured, his breath warm against her neck, 'unless you'd like me to do a lap of honour.'

She stepped smartly out of his grasp. Still trembling from her close encounter with his body, she took the precaution of moving away from him. Goodness, her heart was pumping a mile a minute.

What had made her react to him like that?

'That's it. You've had your five minutes of fame.' Her jokey tone was as fake as her wide smile, but hopefully no one would notice.

'A big round of appreciation for Ken, everyone,' she said. 'He's obviously a very fast learner.'

In response to the ripple of applause that followed, Ken delivered an exaggerated bow. Then, flashing Lisa a wicked smile, he turned and strolled nonchalantly back to his seat.

She would ignore him from now on, she decided, with an angry shake of her head. He thought he was so smart! Well, he'd soon get tired of sitting there by himself and with any luck he'd go home.

★ ★ ★

But it was wishful thinking on her part. Not only was he still hanging around at the end of the session, he also appeared

33

to have a following of attractive young women hanging on his every word.

'I'm surprised you're still here,' she said as the last of her students called goodbye. 'I wouldn't have thought this was your scene.'

He hoisted himself on to the stage and helped her dismantle the equipment. 'I was tempted to leave, I must admit, especially after that impromptu dance demonstration you forced me into.' A corner of his mouth slanted upwards. 'But then my conscience got the better of me and I decided to stay and offer you a lift home.'

'Conscience? That's rich considering that it's your fault I'll soon be out of a job.' She knew she was being petty, but his decision still rankled.

'Give me a break, Lisa.' He reached out to touch her shoulder, but she shrugged it off. 'Look,' he persisted, 'believe it or not, I do have some sympathy with your predicament.'

'But not enough to make you reconsider?'

'Did I say that? Now who's making assumptions?'

Lisa flung the last few CDs into the box and slammed it shut. 'Well, you obviously don't want to talk about it, which speaks volumes.'

'Wrong again.' He caught her arm and turned her round to face him. 'There's actually something I want to discuss with you. But I don't think clearly on an empty stomach, so why don't we grab a bite to eat? You must be starving after all that exercise.'

She gave him a long, hostile look. 'What's there to discuss? You made your feelings perfectly clear back at the hotel.'

'I've had a chance to give it a bit more thought since then . . .'

'And you've realised what, exactly?' She waited for him to continue but he merely raised a corner of his mouth in a tantalising smile.

'Go on,' she prompted. 'You can't leave it there. For goodness' sake, how long does it take to say, 'Lisa, I'll be very happy to reinstate your classes, and see you at the hotel in two weeks time'?'

He gave a loud guffaw, then shook his head. 'Nice try, but you're not catching me that easily. Now, we can either agree to disagree and let the matter end there, or you can join me for a meal and we'll try to sort out the problem. The choice is yours, Lisa. Which is it to be?'

She'd go for the meal, of course. If there was any chance that he might change his mind, then it was in her best interests to be civil to him.

★ ★ ★

It was approaching eleven o'clock when they rolled up at Franco's Spaghetti House, and the place was busy. Luckily there were two vacant seats at a table by the door, and Ken quickly commandeered them both.

'I can recommend the lasagne,' he told her, passing her a menu. 'I often come here when I need a change from hotel food.'

'You live at the hotel?'

'No, I have a flat just far enough away to prevent me from being on twenty-four-hour call.'

'I can understand that. There can't be many wives who'd relish living above the shop — luxury hotel or not.'

Amusement danced in his eyes. 'Never having had one I'm not much of an authority on that, but my mother started married life living at the hotel and it never seemed to bother her.'

What in heaven's name had made her start that thread of conversation? Now he'd think she was trying to find out whether or not he was married, when she really couldn't have cared less.

'Really?' she said, anxious to leave her faux-pas behind her. She unrolled her napkin and smoothed it across her lap with exaggerated care. 'I wouldn't have thought a busy hotel a particularly good place to bring up a child.'

'Me neither,' Ken replied. 'But being

professional ballroom dancers, my parents' main priority was easy access to the hotel ballroom.'

'What?' Astonishment caught in her throat. 'Your parents were professional dancers? No wonder you sailed through that dance so easily! I bet you were trained from the moment you could walk, and have stacks of medals and trophies to prove it.'

He gave a wry smile. 'Yes, to the first part at least. You aren't the first person to set your sights on running dance classes from the hotel. My mother held lessons there for a number of years, and she made sure I was well grounded in all the techniques — '

'I knew it!' Lisa breathed. 'And that's why you weren't keen on line dancing, isn't it?' Her gaze meshed with his as she waited for his confirmation. To someone trained in classic ballroom, line dancing must seem like a poor relation — a hotchpotch of styles and techniques. 'Well, now you've seen there's a lot more to it — '

'But no to the second,' he cut in with firm emphasis. 'There were no trophies. I learned to dance as a child and came to loathe it.'

Her eyes widened. 'But why?'

He heaved a sigh. 'It's a long and not very interesting story.'

'It'll be interesting to me,' she assured him. 'I'm a slow eater.'

'OK then. But don't say I didn't warn you.' Ken closed his eyes for an instant. 'I was an only child and my mother, convinced she'd given birth to a future world champion, put me through my paces from the moment I could stand. The problem was, she didn't bother to ask me my feelings on the matter, and I hated every minute.'

'So what did you do to get out of it?'

'I developed a passion for football.' A nostalgic look came over his face at the memory. 'My father was so proud to see me in the school team that he immediately set about convincing my mother that my time would be better spent on the football field than in the ballroom.'

Lisa rested her chin on her hands. 'Did she take much persuading?'

'On the surface, no, she was amazingly compliant. But every so often she would try to rekindle my interest by finding me little jobs to do at her Saturday night socials.'

She laughed with him at that. 'She sounds a very determined lady.'

'Oh, she was,' he grimaced. 'She had me putting on the music or collecting glasses — anything to keep me in the ballroom.'

'Poor you. Did you hate it?' she asked, resisting the urge to give his hand a comforting squeeze.

He leaned back in his chair and frowned pensively for a moment before shaking his head. 'Looking back, I don't suppose I did. Despite hating the dancing aspect, I enjoyed the social side of things. In fact, it was probably those Saturday night dances that first sparked my interest in the hospitality industry.'

'That should have pleased your father. I bet he was thrilled that his only son wanted to follow in his footsteps.'

'To be honest I think it irritated the hell out of him. He was used to coasting along, doing things in the same old way that they'd been done for years, and when I came into the business, full of ideas, it really did put his back up.'

'That's called the generation gap, isn't it?' Lisa said with a grin. 'So did he sack you?'

'It didn't quite come to that. After a year, I moved to the city to work for a more adventurous employer.'

A small idea sparked in Lisa's mind and grew rapidly. Now was the perfect opportunity to bring up the subject of the ballroom again. But she would have to play it carefully.

'But now you're back and about to put all those innovative ideas into practice, why not take a chance on my classes?' she asked.

He stared at her for an instant. 'What you're doing is hardly innovative, Lisa

— at least, not in my understanding of the word.'

She scrutinised his expression for some indication that he might be teasing her, but saw only quiet contemplation.

'Are you sure you're not letting your personal experience colour your views?' she asked, trying to keep her tone light and casual. 'You could be keeping dancing off the agenda for all the wrong reasons.'

'Not at all.' His response was immediate. 'My personal dislike of the activity has absolutely no bearing on my decision. The bottom line is that, these days, dancing just won't bring in sufficient revenue. My mother's classes ended when her health took a turn for the worse . . . ' He began toying with the cutlery and from the expression on his face Lisa realised that his mother must have died shortly afterwards.

'By then the numbers had fallen off and it was pretty obvious that the activity was on the wane and people no longer wanted to learn to dance.'

Lisa leaned forward. 'But I'm offering a modern, up-to-date approach and I promise you, the interest's there,' she said earnestly.

He raised his eyes to hers. 'From what I've seen tonight I don't doubt it. But what you're offering is totally out of keeping with my vision of the hotel's future and I can't include you in my long-term plans.'

Lisa glared at him. 'So if you're not going to let me use the hotel,' she persisted, 'why did you bother to bring me here?'

'Patience, Lisa,' he chided. 'I was speaking about the long-term — the short term is an entirely different matter.'

They were interrupted by the arrival of their main course and it wasn't until they'd both made short work of a generous helping of lasagne that he put her out of her misery.

'I've decided to offer you use of the ballroom,' he said out of the blue, once he'd mopped up the last drop of sauce from his plate. 'But for — '

'Yes! Oh, Ken — ' she interrupted, bubbling with excitement. 'I promise you won't be sorry. I have so many keen students who want . . . '

He held up his hand. 'Whoa! Hold your horses — I hadn't finished. But for the summer season only. That means you can move in, as arranged, in two weeks' time, provided you agree to be out by the beginning of September.'

Her smile faded. 'I see.'

He studied her face. 'That should go some way towards helping you pay off your loan and give you time to find somewhere else.'

It wasn't exactly what she'd hoped for, but it was better than nothing. And who could tell? Once her classes had proved a success, he might change his mind again and let her stay on indefinitely.

'I agree.' She held out her hand. 'So it's a deal?'

'Except for one thing.'

44

Lisa let her hand drop. She might have known there would be a catch.

'I suppose you're going to ask for a percentage of the takings in addition to me hiring the ballroom?'

'Now there's a thought . . . '

'Forget I said that.'

She scrutinised his face, but his expression gave her no clues. 'Then I bet you want my students to buy all their drinks at the bar instead of — '

He shook his head. 'You know, if you'd slow down for a moment and stop jumping to conclusions we'd be able to sort this out a lot quicker.'

'Sorry.' She made a mental note not to interrupt him again.

He kept her in suspense a few seconds longer, then said, 'I want you to have a DJ working alongside you.'

Lisa's mouth dropped open. 'But — '

'No 'ifs' or 'buts'. You can't possibly run things efficiently as a one-woman band. I want this to be a professional set-up, Lisa. The Cliff Hotel has a reputation to uphold.'

Her heart dipped. How could he do this to her? Build up her hopes and then make his offer conditional on something she couldn't provide?

'I can't afford to pay a DJ,' she admitted with a shaky sigh. 'At least, not until I've paid off my equipment, and that won't be for months.'

He didn't answer. Was he expecting her to beg? Well, career or no career, she was too proud for that.

But it was worth having one last try at convincing him to change his mind. Concentrating on keeping her voice calm and steady, she said in earnest tones. 'I'd make sure it was professional, I promise. I'd get there early, have everything set up . . . '

One look at his face told her he wouldn't budge on this. 'I'm afraid it's non-negotiable,' he said, his words confirming her fears.

'But . . . ' He rested his arms on the table and propped his chin in his hand 'I'm prepared to throw a DJ in as part of the deal, as long as you agree to

46

delegate some of your workload.'

What could she say? If she continued to put forward objections, the deal would be off. 'I — '

'Lisa!'

The familiar voice made her spin round in her seat.

'Philip! What are you doing here?'

Philip glanced from her to Ken then back again. 'Advising Franco,' he said, tapping his briefcase. 'We've just spent the best part of my evening sorting out his V.A.T.' He paused. 'And you?'

Flustered, she gestured over the table. 'Philip, this is Ken Huntley, the new owner of the Cliff Hotel. Philip Davidson.'

As they shook hands she saw Philip's eyes go to Ken's casual attire. 'Ken and I are having a meeting,' she said hastily. 'He isn't happy about me moving my classes to the hotel ballroom, and we're trying to sort out a compromise.'

Philip's smile didn't reach his eyes. He fixed them on Ken. 'It must be a very tricky situation if it can't be sorted out during normal office hours. Or do all your meetings include dinner out?'

'Philip — ' A flush of colour stung her face. Did he think . . . ? Oh no, it wasn't possible. 'Philip, we — '

He put up a hand to silence her. 'I'm just interested in finding out whether this compromise is well within reach, or if Mr Huntley is about to invite you to a nightclub to finish the deal.'

'Oh, I think the discussion is almost over,' Ken said evenly.

Philip put a possessive hand on Lisa's shoulder. The look he gave her excluded Ken. 'Well, I'm about to leave, so if you and Mr Huntley have finished, I'll walk you to your car.'

Lisa half stood, about to explain that her car was stranded outside the Cliff Hotel, when Ken's hand on her arm pulled her down again.

'The meeting's not over yet.' His tone was pleasant but firm. 'I need Lisa to confirm one small, but very necessary, detail before we can wind things up.'

'Really?' Philip's voice was heavy

with irony. 'What might that be?'

Lisa flinched. At his scathing best, her boyfriend was not a particularly pleasant adversary, and despite everything she didn't want Ken to be on the receiving end.

She put out a hand and clutched at his sleeve. 'Philip, I think — '

But once again she wasn't allowed to finish her sentence.

'It was a simple, straightforward enquiry,' Philip persisted, crooking a cynical eyebrow. 'So come on — what small detail exactly?'

Ken leaned back in his seat. 'Lisa needs a DJ. It's a requirement of the contract — and I was just about to offer myself for the position.'

Philip's eyes narrowed. 'You surely don't expect me to believe that? You're no more a DJ than I am.'

'You know, you're right,' Ken returned with easy confidence. 'So why don't I step down and let you fill the vacancy?' His smile broadened. 'Do you have a Stetson and cowboy boots?'

A flicker of unease darted across Philip's face. 'You *are* joking?'

'Not at all,' Ken said, maintaining a neutral tone. 'It's just that a sedate grey suit might be regarded as a tad unadventurous for the DJ scene and I was wondering what we could do to liven up your image.'

'Hey, hold on a minute . . . '

Ken pondered for a moment, then his expression lightened. 'I know! There's a fancy dress shop in the High Street. It's called — '

Philip stiffened. 'You can stop right there. I've better things to do with my time than get togged up as the Rhinestone Cowboy. So if you're up for the role, then please . . . go ahead.'

'Well, if you're sure . . . '

Lisa stared at Ken, aghast. What on earth was he playing at?

'Excuse me, but don't I have a say in any of this?'

Ken placed a gentle hand on her arm. 'Yes, of course. What would you like to add?'

She met his serene expression with one of anger, then turned towards her boyfriend. 'There's no question of you being asked to be DJ,' she said, with a placating smile. 'I know how busy you are and I wouldn't dream of asking you to help out.'

He glanced down at her and his features relaxed.

'Thank heaven for small mercies,' he muttered. 'Not that I wouldn't be capable,' he added, glaring across at Ken once more. 'After all, how difficult can it be to load a few CDs?'

Ken shot him an appreciative smile. 'That's exactly what I was about to say to Lisa — you've taken the words right out of my mouth.'

'In that case, please feel free to finalise your arrangements. I've had a long and arduous day, and to be frank, I'm anxious to get home.'

'Philip, wait — ' Lisa began.

But he'd already opened the door and was striding out into the street.

Philip Is Not Amused

'Thanks a lot!' Lisa hissed as she whirled back to face Ken. 'That's about as helpful as a hole in the head. Once he finds it's not true, he'll be convinced we were out on a date. And you're not the one who'll have to persuade him he's wrong.'

'Don't you think you might be over-reacting a little?'

'Ken, that wasn't just a tiny fib. It was a whopping great lie! What were you thinking?'

'I wasn't lying.' Ken handed his credit card to the waitress with a smile. 'You need a DJ and I have the technical know-how for it. What's wrong with that?'

'Everything! For a start, you don't like dancing!'

'That's right.' He smiled mischievously. 'But unless you feel compelled to use me in another demonstration, I don't expect to do any.'

'Fair enough,' she conceded, inwardly cursing the sudden rush of heat the memory brought to her face. 'But you have a hotel to run, or have you forgotten that?'

'Not for a minute.' He got to his feet and gave her a curiously intimate smile as he held out a hand to help her up.

Lisa reluctantly placed her hand in his. Strong warm fingers curled around hers, sending tiny tingles dancing up her arm and a new wave of heat to her face. What was wrong with her? She didn't even like the man and here she was turning all pink-cheeked whenever he touched her.

'It's not good for a manager to spend all his time tucked away in an office,' he said, guiding her through the packed tables to the cash desk.

'So, get out more,' Lisa retorted. 'I've already told you that.'

He gave a low chuckle. 'I'm talking from a purely business point of view here — and despite what you might think, I'm not short of things to do in my leisure time.'

He was standing close to her and his warm breath touching her temples was doing strange things to her insides.

'Even so, there must be hundreds of things you'd rather do than DJ for a line dance class,' she persisted. 'What about that enormous pile of paperwork you have waiting for you back at your office?'

He collected his credit card from the waitress and returned it to his wallet.

'That should only take a couple more weeks,' he assured Lisa as they walked out into the cool, night air. 'And then I'd like some contact with my customers. A spell in the ballroom would fit the bill and do wonders for public relations.'

For his ego, more like, Lisa thought.

'In fact — ' he paused as he unlocked his car ' — I might even follow it with a spell as a waiter or doorman, or some time behind the bar.'

'It sounds to me as if you're craving a less responsible job,' Lisa retorted. 'Is the novelty of being manager beginning to wear a bit thin?'

He looked unperturbed. 'Not a chance. I love my job — and all its responsibilities.' He walked round the car and got into the driver's seat.

Lisa stared at him. 'Then why would you want to do all these . . . menial tasks, when you don't have to?'

'Because working at grass roots level is an excellent way to gauge customer satisfaction and improve the quality of service.'

Well, that made sense, she admitted. But working *with* him wasn't the same as working *for* him. She only hoped he understood the difference.

★　★　★

Other than issuing Ken with directions to her flat, Lisa had very little to say after that. Perhaps she was feeling overwhelmed by the turn of events, he decided. He'd certainly given her plenty of food for thought.

Ken was feeling a little dazed himself, for that matter. Whatever had caused him to change his mind about offering her the use of the hotel ballroom? Had those mesmerising eyes of hers hypnotised him?

'We ought to get together sometime over the next two weeks,' he told her as he pulled up outside her flat. 'To discuss our play list.'

'*Our* play list?' Lisa echoed, emphasising the first word with a measure of sarcasm. 'Surely that's my decision?'

Ken ignored the indignation in her voice. 'Yes, of course, but I'm new to this job, so it would help me if I had some idea of the order of play.'

She seemed to give it some thought.

'I'll write you a list,' she said, as she climbed out of the car. 'And we'll go through it a few minutes before the start of the class. Now, if there's nothing else, I'll say thank you for dinner, and I'll see you at my class in two weeks' time.'

He chuckled to himself as she walked to the gate. She was on her dignity again, no doubt due to him teasing that pompous boyfriend of hers. Or it could be to do with the fact that she wasn't keen on having a sidekick foisted on her. Well, either way, she'd have to get used to it.

'Aren't you forgetting something, Lisa?' he called after her.

She paused to glance over her shoulder. 'No, I don't think so.'

Ken grinned. 'Don't worry — I didn't mean a goodnight kiss.'

He could hear her sharp intake of breath from where he stood.

'It's just that your music system's still in the boot,' he explained. 'Hang on a moment and I'll get it out for you.'

She murmured a slightly chastened 'Thanks' as she returned to the car. He snatched a sidelong glance at her, hoping to catch the glimmer of a smile, but her expression was thoughtful rather than amused. In fact, standing there silently beneath the pale glow of the amber streetlight, she looked more like a delicate figure from a pre-Raphaelite painting than the feisty young go-getter he'd battled with previously.

With some reluctance he dragged his gaze back to the contents of the boot. He handed over her Stetson followed by the case of CDs, then picked up the sound system and accompanied her back to the house.

She hovered awkwardly on the doorstep. 'I'd invite you in for coffee, but . . . ' Her tone was apologetic.

'That's quite all right — I understand.' His smile was sincere. 'I'll just drop this inside your front door and then be on my way before the neighbours can so much as twitch a curtain.'

He was as good as his word.

'A goodnight kiss!' Lisa repeated to herself, still warm with embarrassment. As if such a silly idea would ever have entered her head!

'Come on, Philip,' Lisa coaxed. 'I've explained why I was out with Ken last night, and you said that you understood.'

Philip got up from her kitchen table and helped himself to another cup of coffee.

'I do,' he said grumpily, 'but what I can't understand is why you're bothering to move to the hotel at all. If this Ken Huntley character can't offer you any more than a six-week contract, why not wind up the classes now and be done with it? You've just finished a business studies course, for heaven's sake — you'll easily find a job in an office.'

'Oh, Philip, please! Working in an office would bore me rigid — I can't think of anything I'd hate more.'

'So why take the course in the first place? There's no logic in that.'

She dropped her mug into the sink and walked over to join him.

'When I enrolled on the course I'd always intended to go back home the minute it was over to help my mother run her children's dance school. A career in business has never held the slightest attraction for me — unless it was my own business.'

He looked surprised. 'You never said . . . '

'The idea sort of got shelved when I started dating you,' she murmured, smiling up at him. 'Although it's not too late to go back to my original idea — my mother left the offer open indefinitely.'

'I've a better suggestion.' He dropped a kiss on her forehead. 'Why not open a children's dance school here in Sandford? You could work from smaller premises and tell Ken Huntley to stick his stupid ballroom.'

'It's not that simple.' She sighed. 'This town has all the dance schools it needs. Most of them have been running for years and virtually have the monopoly — like my mother's back home.'

'I see.'

She looked anxiously into his eyes, wanting him to understand.

'But line dancing — that's a different matter entirely. Nobody else was doing it when I first came here, and since then I've managed to build up a dedicated following. Once Ken Huntley has spent some time working alongside me, he'll soon realise — '

'About that . . . ' Philip cut in, a serious look crossing his features. 'Do you realise you'll be seeing nearly as much of him as you do of me?'

'So?' She tilted her head to one side.

'I suppose I'm worried he might come between us.'

Lisa suppressed a smile. Philip was jealous!

It was sweet of him to admit it, but he had absolutely nothing to worry about. She had no romantic interest in Ken Huntley whatsoever.

She leaned her head on his shoulder. 'Not a chance,' she whispered. 'I don't like the arrangement any more than you do. But once the hotel is refurbished and I'm a permanent fixture, Ken Huntley will have far more important things to occupy his time than playing DJ.'

It was then that she remembered her car. Without it she'd be hard pushed to honour her temporary contract, never mind a permanent one.

'By the way, when can your mechanic take a look at my car?'

He stiffened. 'This is getting to be a bit regular, Lisa. The arrangement was that K.P. Motors would keep my car on the road in exchange for me doing their books. Your car was never part of the deal.'

'Please, Philip.' She turned to lift the telephone receiver from the wall. 'It's not a huge task — your car hardly ever goes wrong.'

With a long-suffering sigh, Philip took the receiver from her and keyed in the number. 'Keith? It's Philip Davidson . . . '

Lisa sidled up to him and leaned her

head against the receiver so that she could hear their conversation.

'Yes!' she yelled when the unseen Keith offered to send somebody out at two o'clock that afternoon.

Philip winced, but Lisa ignored it and gave him a grateful hug.

'Thanks, Philip. Now, if I start lunch right away, we can easily be at the hotel for two.'

He eased himself out of her embrace. 'I'm sorry, but I won't be able to come with you. I've a fitting for a new suit this afternoon.'

'Oh.' Her smile faltered slightly. 'But you'll stay for lunch?'

He looked uneasy. 'Actually, my mother's expecting me home. I promised to drop her at the hairdresser's on my way into town and she thought it would be nice if we ate together.'

Lisa made an effort to hide her annoyance. 'Well then . . . shall I see you tonight as usual?'

He placed an arm around her shoulders. 'Of course,' he murmured, bending to kiss her. 'But now, I've got to go. Mother's preparing a special prawn and mussel risotto, and I promised I wouldn't be late.'

She could hardly blame him, Lisa thought as she waved him off; ham sandwiches, however lovingly prepared, were no match for one of his mother's elaborate concoctions. Maybe she ought to take a leaf out of her book and develop a few culinary skills of her own.

But first things first. She dashed back into the kitchen and gave the coffee cups a quick rinse under the tap. As much as she'd like to cook Philip a romantic meal, it came well down on her 'things to do' list, and stood no chance of making it to the top for the next two weeks at least.

★ ★ ★

The mechanic closed the bonnet of her car and wiped his hands on a piece of oily rag.

'It doesn't look good. Have you

64

thought about buying a new one?'

Lisa's heart sank.

'Please don't write it off yet,' she pleaded. 'It'll be weeks before I can afford to replace it, and I need it for my job.'

He rubbed the back of his neck. 'I suppose I could take it back to the garage and let the boss have a look at it.' He ran his fingers over a patch of corroded paintwork. 'But he'll probably say it's not worth the hassle. We've scrapped cars in much better nick than this.'

This called for desperate measures.

'Look, if it's a complicated job I wouldn't expect you to fix it for nothing. Tell Keith I'll pay whatever he asks, just as long as it's back on the road for Tuesday.'

'All right, we'll take it in and see what we can do.'

It's a good thing Ken Huntley's not around to witness this, Lisa thought, glancing nervously around the car park. If she hoped to convince him that she could present a classy enough image for his new, upmarket hotel, the last thing he needed to see was her dilapidated old car being towed from the premises.

So why did she experience a hazy feeling of regret when it became obvious he was nowhere around? I suppose part of me was hoping he might pop up and offer me a lift, she decided as she trudged wearily towards the bus stop. What other reason could there possibly be?

★   ★   ★

By six o'clock on Tuesday evening, the car was back on the road, and to Lisa's relief, it took her straight to her class without any problems.

All she had to do now, she reflected as she made up the drinks for the interval, was announce the change of venue, hand deliver her fliers and give the local newspaper the go-ahead to run her advertisement.

But despite meeting her targets with

a couple of days to spare, Lisa didn't sleep well the night before the transfer. What if half her regulars had chosen this week to go on holiday, and no newcomers turned up?

Then you'll just have to persuade Ken Huntley that it's a temporary glitch, she told herself firmly. You've done all you can to ensure a trouble-free transfer. The chances are everything will go smoothly.

No such luck. Less than an hour before her debut, Lisa's car spluttered to a halt at the end of her street and refused to start.

Don't panic, she told herself. It wasn't yet seven o'clock. With any luck there'd be somebody at K. P. Motors. If she phoned straightaway, Keith might send a mechanic.

She sprinted back up the street to her flat.

'Keith? It's Lisa Gates,' she began with determined brightness. 'Sorry to bother you again so soon, but my car won't start.'

'I can't say I'm surprised,' came the testy response. 'It's a miracle it's lasted as long as it has.'

She took a calming breath. 'I realise that, but can you please send somebody out to fix it?

'Listen, love. It's terminal. Beyond recovery. As a favour to Philip I'll tow it to the scrap yard, but other than that I can't help you.'

Her heart plummeted. She'd expected a few scathing comments but not for one moment had she imagined she'd be left without any transport.

'But I'm stranded here without a car and can't get to my appointment!'

'Sorry, love. You'll have to give one of the taxi firms a call.'

If only it were that simple. After paying the garage, she had barely enough money to put food on the table let alone hire a taxi.

There was nothing else for it — she would have to ring Philip.

* * *

'I suppose you'll want me to pick you up again at half-past ten,' he grumbled as he dropped her in the hotel car park. 'Assuming, of course, that I've finished with my client by then.'

'That's right,' she said sweetly, 'and a little more sympathy wouldn't go amiss — it's not often I call on you to help out.'

'And when you do, you certainly pick your moments.' He heaved a sigh. 'Ten minutes before I'm due to meet a client I find myself pushing your car off the road, then chauffeuring you to the other end of the town.'

'I'm worth it though, aren't I?' she said, searching his face for signs of a smile. 'And when your client realises that your girlfriend's business was at stake, I'm sure he won't mind you being a few minutes late.'

He sent her a rueful grin. 'It's not the lateness that worries me as much as my appearance — look at the state of me!'

'I'm sorry, Philip,' she said, brushing a patch of dust from his shoulder. 'It's very considerate of you to go to so much trouble. I'll see you at half-past ten.'

'Come on, I'll give you a hand carrying in your equipment,' he said, to her surprise. 'I dare say my client can wait another five minutes.'

The First Class With Ken

The doorman held the door and waved them in with a welcoming smile.

'Lisa, slow down, will you?' Philip panted from behind. 'This stuff isn't light.'

At the sound of his voice a tall, broad-shouldered figure in a black Stetson broke away from a group at the entrance to the ballroom.

'Here, let me . . . ' he said smoothly, whisking the sound system from Philip's grasp. 'We're running out of time.'

Ken! Her thanks froze on her lips as she recognised him. Whatever was he wearing?

The Stetson she had no problems with, nor the dark jeans with the sturdy leather belt. But his shirt was a different matter entirely. Mustard yellow and covered in red and brown guitar motifs, the fabric would have looked more at home on a duvet cover in a ten-year-old's bedroom.

'I see you're admiring my shirt,' he said with a disarming smile. 'It took some finding, but I think you'll agree it was well worth the effort.'

The glint in his eyes suggested otherwise. This shirt was nothing more than a ploy to push him into the limelight, Lisa concluded. But she could be wrong, of course, so she decided that her best option for the moment was to gloss over the matter and not risk saying anything that might cause friction.

'It looks . . . ' She cast around for the right words.

'Like a guitar pizza,' Philip said with a superior little smile. 'Maybe there's something to be said for a sedate grey suit after all.'

'You say the sweetest things,' Ken murmured. 'Now if you'll excuse us, Lisa and I have a lot to do and not much time left to do it.'

Lisa bristled. 'I suppose that was a

dig at me?' she hissed as she followed him into the ballroom. 'I don't make a habit of arriving at the last minute. Tonight was strictly a one-off.'

'Are you sure about that?' he answered. 'Only I seem to remember you having trouble getting to your last class on time as well.'

She was hurrying to keep up with him. 'That was a one-off, too. Look, I've been late twice in three years — I reckon that's pretty good going myself, so would you please let the matter drop?'

He paused at the steps to the stage. 'Really, Lisa, you'll have to learn to control that temper of yours. You get angry faster than anyone I've ever met. I was merely hinting to Philip that it was time he left — I wasn't criticising you.'

'No?'

'No. So you're a few minutes late. What does it matter, now you've a DJ to help you set everything up?'

She followed him up the steps. 'That

one small advantage hardly justifies me having a permanent DJ.'

'There are others, I assure you.'

'Really? Personally, I can't think of any.'

He took her flag and draped it over a table set out at the front of the stage.

'Well, for a start it means you can leave me to set this lot up while you spend a few minutes relaxing over the drink I left for you at the bar.'

'You left me a drink?' she repeated. His amiability confused her. 'Why would you bother doing that?'

He shrugged. 'When I realised you'd been delayed, I thought you'd like an iced drink when you eventually managed to get here.'

'Thanks, but I don't drink when I'm teaching. I like to keep a clear head.'

'Very wise,' he agreed. 'But it's a lime and lemon, not a shot of whisky, so why don't you nip off and take advantage of it while I finish off up here?'

It was a tempting thought, but not a very practical one.

'Thanks, but I'd better get over to the door and start collecting the money. People will be getting restless waiting out in the foyer, especially now they've seen me arrive.'

He grabbed her shoulders and spun her round to face the door.

'It's all taken care of. One of my employees is issuing tickets. I don't think anyone will mind if you take a few minutes to go and cool down.'

Cool down? Was he implying she was in a foul temper? She whirled back to face him, but his expression held nothing but concern.

'Go on — you look as if you could do with a few minutes to yourself. I've had my share of unreliable cars and I understand what a hassle they can be.'

'Who said anything about my car?'

He grinned. 'You didn't have to. The accountant obviously wasn't here for the dancing, so I assumed he'd been drafted in as a last-minute chauffeur.'

'He had,' she admitted. 'I don't know what I'd have done without him.'

'But you're here now, and that's all that matters. So go and have that drink, and put the whole experience behind you.'

Having a sidekick did have its advantages, she conceded — especially one so adept at anticipating her needs. A few minutes out was exactly what she needed, loath as she was to admit it.

She gave herself ten minutes and then headed straight back across the ballroom to the stage.

Ken had set everything up, and was now standing at the edge of the dance floor, regaling a group of her younger dancers with some amusing anecdote.

'Time to start,' she called out as she walked past them. 'But before we put on any music, can we start with a quick check on the head-mike, please?'

He didn't appear to have heard her.

'Ken?'

He turned round. 'Sorry,' he said, sauntering over to meet her. 'Were you talking to me?'

'If you can manage to prise yourself

away from your fan club for a few minutes, I need you to run a sound check.'

'Sorry, ladies,' he called. 'We'll have to finish our chat later.'

They gave a collective groan and settled themselves at the table closest to the stage.

No need to ask what they thought of her DJ,. Lisa thought wryly — that was all too evident from their love-struck expressions. But was it really necessary for him to stand around flirting with them when she was ready to start the class?

'I realise you've other things you'd rather be doing,' Lisa snapped as she mounted the steps to the stage, 'but as you've already pointed out, we're fast running out of time.'

He paused at the steps and glanced quickly round the room.

'It wouldn't hurt to wait another ten minutes or so. There aren't that many here at the moment.'

Anger simmered along her nerves.

Just listen to him! Anyone would think he was her business advisor instead of a mere assistant. He might own the hotel, but he knew little about running a dance class and could keep his half-baked opinions to himself.

'We can't do that. The class was advertised to begin at half-past seven, so that's the time it has to start.'

'I shouldn't think anyone would mind if we delayed it a while. There are still quite a few people filtering in.'

Lisa continued up the steps.

'Lisa, think about it,' he went on, following close behind. 'If you start now while the ballroom's half empty, the class will have no atmosphere.'

Lisa paused at the edge of the stage to glare at him. 'And if I don't deliver exactly what I promised, people will feel short-changed and won't bother coming again,' she pointed out. 'Or maybe that's what you want to happen? Consistently low numbers would give you more than enough reason to close the classes down before

September, wouldn't it?'

He picked up the headset and held it out.

'Lisa, the room is yours until September, whatever your numbers, and I'm sorry if you mistook my suggestions for interference.'

Suggestions. There he went again, acting as if he were a font of knowledge and she the floundering apprentice. She didn't need his suggestions, for heaven's sake. When would he realise that?

'So . . . if it was only a suggestion,' she said, clipping the battery unit on to her belt, 'then you won't mind if I ignore it, right?'

'Of course not,' he answered, unruffled. 'That's the whole point of suggestions — nobody's compelled to take them on board.'

She pressed her advantage. 'Then that's what I'll do, if it's all the same to you. I'm in charge of this class and I say it starts on time.'

'In that case, let's steam ahead.' He flicked a switch on the sound system.

'Give me a quick count to three while I check the sound.'

She'd expected more of a protest. Suddenly she found herself standing in the centre of the stage feeling unbearably mean.

*　*　*

The feeling didn't last long. Fifteen minutes into the session, she was ready to announce the next dance when a deep masculine voice reverberated around the ballroom.

'Hi, everyone. Lisa seems to have forgotten to introduce me, so I thought I'd pitch in and explain who I am and what I'm doing here.'

'I don't remember giving you a microphone,' she cut in the second he'd completed his introduction. 'So now that we know who you are, perhaps you'd like to put it back where you found it and concentrate on supplying the music.'

He hung his head and affected such a

woebegone expression that the room echoed with murmurs of sympathy.

If only they knew what a ruthless business mind lurked behind that affable exterior, Lisa thought, they would soon realise their sympathy was misplaced.

He gave the dancers a beseeching look. 'All together. Ahhhhh . . . '

What was she to do? Her students clearly thought this little spat was something she and Ken had set up to provide some light-hearted amusement. To insist on him relinquishing his microphone now would cast her in the role of wicked witch.

'Oh, all right,' she said grudgingly. 'I suppose you can keep it.'

'Thanks,' he said. 'But if I might continue on a more serious note — we hope you all enjoy dancing here over the next few weeks, but we do have to ask you not to carry drinks across the dance floor. Spills can be lethal on a floor like this, and we don't want anyone slipping and injuring themselves.'

A reasonable enough request, Lisa told herself, and considering the safety aspects, one she ought to have made herself. And I probably would, if he'd given me the chance. Ken Huntley was taking far too much upon himself and she'd be telling him so before the evening was out.

But first she'd have to catch him. After announcing the next track, he promptly left the stage and vanished into the sea of dancers. A quick scan of the room produced no positive sightings, until towards the end of the dance Lisa spotted him sitting at a table of elderly women, deep in conversation with an elegant newcomer.

He just can't help himself, Lisa thought, jumping down from the stage and moving towards their table. Old or young, a woman only has to smile at him and he's at her side in the blink of an eye.

No wonder he'd offered his services as a DJ. The man clearly needed constant excitement and challenge. It was pathetic, really, she thought.

'Hello, you must be one of my new ones,' Lisa said, breezing up to his companion. 'Are you enjoying yourself?'

Ken looked startled at the intrusion. 'Lisa, meet Yvette,' he said. 'She was just remarking on how many people turned up after the class had started.'

Lisa shook Yvette's hand. 'Yes, there were quite a few,' she acknowledged, giving Ken a sweet smile. 'And if this is your way of saying I told you so, I'm very pleased to have been proved wrong.'

'Nothing gets past you, does it?' he answered, placing a hand on her shoulder and steering her back towards the dance floor. 'But much as I'd like to, there's no time to sit around chatting. That CD must be nearly at an end by now.'

'Nice meeting you, Yvette,' Lisa called out over her shoulder.

It wasn't until she was back on stage and well into the next dance that Lisa realised she'd been expertly manipulated. By cutting short her chat with Yvette, Ken had once again managed to give the impression that he was the one in charge.

* * *

Lisa didn't get the chance to speak with Yvette again. Each time she tried to snatch a few minutes to finish their chat, Ken called her back to the stage to count-in a group of struggling beginners, or find a CD that he'd managed to misplace. She seethed. How would he like it if she kept finding him tasks to complete whenever he felt like a spot of socialising?

But she needn't have worried. At the end of the evening, Yvette made a point of seeking her out, and congratulated her on a thoroughly enjoyable night out.

'When my husband died I thought my dancing days were over,' the woman told her with a tremor in her voice. 'But I love the idea of being able to come here without a partner and still spend the whole evening dancing.'

'So many other people have told me the same thing,' Lisa answered, warming to her at once. 'That's the beauty of line dancing — everyone can dance at their own level and nobody has to find a partner.'

'It seems such a shame that you're only going to be here for the summ season. Have you anywhere lined up the winter?'

Lisa shook her head. 'I'm looking, of course, but I doubt I'll find anywhere as suitable as this. It's exactly what I've been looking for.'

Yvette gave a sympathetic nod. 'Don't give up hope just yet. With a bit of luck you might end up being able to stay here after all.'

'Not a snowball in hell's chance,' came Ken's firm voice, causing Lisa to whirl round with a start.

What was he doing, creeping up on them like that — and more to the point, what made him think he had the right to be so rude to Yvette?

Yvette was evidently of the same mind.

'I wasn't talking to you,' she said, fixing him with a penetrating glare. 'This was supposed to be a private conversation.'

'That's right,' Lisa chipped in. 'Didn't your mother ever tell you it's ᴅ le to butt into other people's versations?'

My mother was hardly ever around,' ᴇ answered affecting an anguished expression, 'so, sadly, some of my social skills are severely lacking.'

'Do I hear violins?' Lisa muttered, not feeling the least bit sympathetic.

Yvette threw her a conspiratorial glance.

'In that case, Ken, you won't mind if Lisa and I try to remedy the situation. Lesson one — private conversations are exactly that, so will you please leave us to finish this chat on our own?'

'Ouch!' he said with a sheepish grin. 'That puts me in my place.'

He turned to Lisa and gave a little bow. 'Excuse me for interrupting, but there's a group of dancers by the stage who'd like to know if you have any spare instruction sheets. The ones you put out seem to have gone, and I don't know where you keep your spares.'

'I'll go and get some more,' Lisa told him, secretly amused at the way Yvette had called him to order. 'Will you excuse me, Yvette?'

Yvette gave an understanding smile and the next time Lisa glanced in her direction she and Ken appeared to have put their differences aside and were deep in conversation once more.

He was lucky the woman had been so forgiving, Lisa thought as she retrieved a folder of dance sheets from under her case of CDs. It's more than she would have done! But then, she understood something of the calculating personality behind that deadly charm. That sympathetic friendliness of his was all an illusion, a mere technique to get people on his side. In fact, if his present career should ever fail, Lisa could imagine him earning a living as a con artist or used car salesman.

'Here we are,' she said, handing out the instruction sheets to the waiting group 'Sorry — I didn't realise I hadn't put enough out.'

'That's all right,' one of them assured her. 'We're glad you still have some — your young man didn't think you had any left.'

Ken, her young man? Lisa gave a light laugh. 'Oh, Ken isn't my boyfriend — he's just helping me out.'

The women exchanged knowing looks, but didn't pursue the matter.

Irritated and a little embarrassed, Lisa decided that from now on she would speak to Ken only when absolutely necessary. That way, no-one would have any reason to think that theirs was anything other than a practical business arrangement.

★   ★   ★

It hadn't been a bad turn-out, Ken thought as he helped Lisa pack everything away.

'It went well, don't you think?' he ventured, bemused by her icy manner.

'Yes, no thanks to you.'

He gave her a startled look. 'What do you mean by that?'

She pushed a wayward strand of curly hair inside her hat, and regarded him with a weary expression. 'Come on, Ken. You know exactly what I mean. So stop playing the innocent and admit it.'

She wasn't giving him much to go on, but if he wanted to enjoy these next few weeks, he'd have to find out what was bothering her. Perhaps the humorous touch would work.

'It's the shirt, right? You didn't like it, did you?' he began, watching her face for any signs of a thaw.

No reply, and not so much as a hint of amusement in her eyes. No matter, he'd just keep chatting until she responded.

'That's easily remedied. I'll take the rest of the batch back to the store and exchange them for something more subdued.'

'It's a pity I can't do the same with you,' she mumbled at last.

His eyebrows shot up. He hadn't been expecting that.

'What do you mean? What have I done?'

At last she opened up. 'I didn't plan on you having your own microphone for starters,' she said. 'But somehow you managed to get hold of one, and forced me into accepting it — and then you used it to summon me to the stage every time I tried to chat with my students.'

Not every time, he thought — just when she'd appeared to be heading towards Yvette.

'I can see that that might have been a bit irritating — '

She hadn't finished. 'However, it was all right for you to disappear from the stage for the same reason, only fifteen minutes into the class.'

Absolutely right. He was guilty as charged, and had no valid excuse to offer — at least, not one he wanted Lisa to hear. How could he explain that when he'd spotted his mother on the dance floor, his only thought had been to get to her fast and persuade her to keep a low profile?

'And whisking me away from Yvette the minute I showed up at your side definitely wasn't on. You made me feel like a skiving schoolkid who needed to be escorted back to class.'

All he'd been trying to do was keep Lisa and his mother apart. At least until he'd had a chance to explain to his mother why he couldn't offer Lisa's classes a permanent home at the hotel. But he'd barely had a chance to plead his case when Lisa had turned up beside them.

'That really wasn't my intention — '

'Maybe not, but that's how it came across. And while we're on the subject of high-handed attitudes, what did you think you were doing barging in on my discussion with Yvette? She made an innocent remark, and she didn't deserve such a put-down.'

Oh, but she did. From the expression on his mother's face at the end of the evening it had been only too clear what she'd been thinking. Dancing had been absent from the hotel for too long, and she longed to see it brought back. If he hadn't intervened when he had, she'd have been urging Lisa to stand her ground, organising a support group and all manner of other things.

He'd go and see her tomorrow and have another try at convincing her that nostalgia wasn't sufficient grounds for cancelling his refurbishments.

But for now, his most pressing problem was how to convince Lisa that he hadn't deliberately set out to sabotage her class.

'You're right. I shouldn't have butted in, but I've explained to her why it was such a sore point and done my best to smooth things out.'

'So what did you say? That your father made an unfortunate decision and you couldn't honour it for more than a few weeks?'

That would have gone down really well, Ken thought, fighting to keep a straight face.

'I simply explained to her that she'd touched on a sensitive subject, and apologised for my sharp response.'

'And she forgave you — just like that?'

He smiled at her incredulous expression. 'I daresay my consummate charm had a lot to do with it — either that or my striking good looks.'

She unclipped her battery pack and removed her headset.

'I think you'll find I'm not swayed by such matters.'

Didn't he know it!

'Would it help if I were to grovel?'

Her mouth quirked. 'That would depend on what you had in mind.'

'How about another visit to Franco's? His food is well worth a second visit . . . even a third and fourth.'

'Now you're getting carried away.'

'Just one visit then, to apologise for us getting off on the wrong foot.'

She picked up her case of CDs and tucked the remaining dance sheets under her arm.

'Nice try, but I really don't think so. Philip's due to pick me up at any minute, and I doubt if he'd appreciate the gesture.'

Drat. He'd forgotten about the accountant. Get him in here voicing his opinions and this little disagreement could escalate into a major fall-out.

Ken lifted the sound system on to the floor and began folding up the flag.

'Some other time then,' he said, searching his mind for something he could do to get things back on a friendly footing.

She picked up her case of CDs.

'If that offer to grovel still stands, I could do with someone to carry the sound system over to Philip's car.'

Without a word, he did as she asked.

He'd been intending to offer, but if it would help her to think he was grovelling . . .

This is more like it, Lisa thought, as he followed her out of the building. Anyone seeing Ken walking a respectful five paces behind her couldn't possibly be left in any doubt as to which of them was the boss.

That was the way things would be from now on, too. She'd treat him with the calm aloofness of an employer addressing an employee. And if he persisted in stepping out of line, then she'd just have to take a leaf out of his book and very publicly call him to heel.

She turned to ask him to set the sound system down and leave her to wait for Philip. But instead of being right behind her, as she'd expected, he was loitering in the doorway chatting to a lingering group of dancers.

At her approach they began drifting away, but she was careful to bid them a pleasant goodnight, despite her sudden irritation.

'There's no need to build up a fan base,' she hissed at him.

'I'm only showing an interest in our customers. My mother did manage to teach me the importance of speaking to everyone in the class at least once during the evening — and her classes were always packed.'

'Mine will be too, when the word gets round. Now, if you'd like to put the sound system down here, I'm sure Philip won't be — '

But before she could say any more she was interrupted by one of her dancers rushing towards her, brandishing a large sheet of paper.

'Lisa, you're not going to like this! I found this flyer on my car windscreen.'

What Else Can Go Wrong?

As Lisa began reading, she felt her heart plummet. 'I don't believe it! Another instructor is offering classes on exactly the same days as mine, at the leisure centre across the road.'

'And they're cheaper, too,' the woman pointed out, as Ken read the leaflet over Lisa's shoulder. 'Can you believe the cheek? They're on every car in the car park. But don't worry.' She patted Lisa's arm. 'I'm sure everyone will be back next week as usual.'

'But will they?' Lisa whispered, as the woman walked back to her car. 'They might say that now, but at these ridiculously low prices, it's only a matter of time before they switch classes.'

Ken placed a hand on her shoulder.

'If you want my opinion — '

She whirled to face him. 'Your opinion? Why on earth should I want that? It's your fault that I'm in this mess.'

His eyebrows shot up. 'How do you work that one out?'

'You're responsible for what goes on at this hotel!' She crumpled the flyer and hurled it to the ground. 'If your security system wasn't so lax, people couldn't walk in off the street and do something like this.'

'And if you'd thought about using the sports hall yourself,' he shot back, 'this predicament wouldn't even exist.'

'Me? Use the leisure centre? Why would I want to do that? I need soft lights, a proper dance floor, and decent acoustics. A huge, echoing sports hall is no use to me. Credit me with some business sense, please.'

'Oh, but I do,' he answered, placing his hands on her shoulders. 'Which is why these new classes don't pose a threat.'

'W-what do you mean,' she mumbled, trying hard not to cry.

'From what I've seen so far, your classes are second to none. And if I weren't so certain they wouldn't fit the hotel's new image, I'd have absolutely no hesitation in keeping you on.'

She felt a small glimmer of hope. 'Really?'

'Really. And I'm convinced you won't lose any pupils to an inferior set-up, no matter how cheap the price.'

'But some people are bound to want to try it,' she choked. 'What happens if . . . ?' Suddenly she couldn't hold back the tears any longer.

'Hey . . . ' he whispered, his arms going round her. 'I thought we'd just agreed you had no competition here?'

'We can't . . . be sure,' she said between sobs. 'What will I do?'

'The best thing you can do right now is go home and get a good night's sleep. If in the morning you still think you've serious cause for concern, come and see me at the hotel, and we'll work out some ideas for extra publicity.'

'It's not ideas I'm short of,' she sobbed. 'I need to put up more posters, run more adverts, deliver more flyers . . .'

'None of which you can afford,' he said softly. 'But what I have in mind won't cost anything. Call in tomorrow and let's talk it over.'

His voice was gentle and reassuring and as his soothing tones washed over her, she felt herself beginning to unwind. She'd been wrong to think of him as totally unscrupulous. He had a kind, protective streak, and . . .

'Lisa,' he murmured, 'as much as I'm enjoying this little display of affection, don't you think you ought to be making a move towards Philip's car? He doesn't strike me as the sort of person who'd appreciate being kept waiting while his girlfriend's in a clinch with another man.'

'Philip!' She'd forgotten all about him for a moment. 'Where is he?' she squealed, pulling away. 'Why didn't you tell me he was here?'

Ken gave a throaty laugh. 'A car's just pulled into the car park. It's too far away to tell who's driving it. But feel free to carry on burrowing into my neck if you like, until we know for certain who it is.'

Heat flooding her cheeks, she snatched up her case of CDs and strode out of the shadows. What on earth had she been thinking, cuddling up to Ken like that? She only hoped Philip hadn't seen her.

But she needn't have worried. Philip was far too weary to take much notice of anything. After a mumbled greeting, he sat yawning in the car while Lisa and Ken carried the sound system and CDs to the boot.

'Has he lost the use of his legs?' Ken asked.

Lisa glared at him. 'I expect he's exhausted. He's just finished three hours' overtime.'

Ken followed her round to the passenger door. 'Speaking as someone who works a twelve-hour day, I don't know how he manages it.'

'My heart goes out to you,' she said, her voice saccharine sweet. 'But you can't really class the last three hours as work — you spent the bulk of them flirting.'

'Now why do the words 'pot' and 'kettle' come to mind?' he murmured, pulling open the door.

She shot him a warning glance as she got in. 'Goodnight, Ken.'

'Goodnight, Lisa. If you drop by around half-past eleven tomorrow, we'll have our little chat over coffee in the hotel restaurant.'

Trust him to make it sound as though they'd planned a cosy date, Lisa fumed. It was a business meeting, that was all — and they wouldn't be talking about anything they couldn't discuss at the start of her next class.

She was on the point of saying as much when a heavy sigh from Philip prompted her to close the door.

'A difficult evening?' she asked, as

she fastened her seat belt.

'Let's just say I'll be pleased to get home. It's been a long day.'

'For you and me both,' Lisa said, preparing to launch into a rundown of her own mini-disasters. 'I got nowhere near the turn-out I was expecting, then when I went into the car park to wait for you — '

'Ah, yes, about that . . . '

Lisa tensed. He'd seen her snuggling up to Ken! How on earth would she explain that away?

'The thing is, if you're relying on me for lifts over the coming weeks, I'm afraid I won't be able to help out.'

Relief washed over her. 'Oh, that's all right. If I hadn't been desperate, I wouldn't have troubled you tonight.'

'That's what I was hoping. One of the partners rang while I was with my client tonight. It turns out that the audit senior for a team he sent over to Manchester has had to return home, and I've been asked to take his place. I'll be home at the weekend, of course, but come Monday morning I'll be heading back to Manchester for another week.'

Lisa smothered a sigh. What a day this had been — and just when she'd decided things couldn't possibly get any worse, Philip had to go and drop a bombshell like that.

He glanced at her. 'You're not saying much.'

What was there to say? It wasn't as if he had any choice in the matter. Unless, like her, you were lucky enough to be your own boss, going where the firm sent you was part and parcel of working life.

'Don't worry. I understand,' she told him. 'You can't be in two places at once — '

'Exactly. And if you don't manage to get another car sorted out, you might be able to strike a deal with one of the taxi firms.'

'I'll bear that in mind,' she told him, not bothering to add that with no spare cash to speak of, both options were out of the question.

Her only alternative was to ask Ken if she could store her equipment somewhere at the hotel — there was surely plenty of room. Then she could travel by bus.

It looked as though she'd be keeping that appointment with Ken tomorrow after all. But she'd be sure to keep things on a business footing; no teasing banter, no crying on his shoulder, and certainly no morning coffee in the hotel restaurant!

With an effort, she dragged her attention back to what Philip was saying.

'So, as we won't be seeing each other until the weekend,' Philip was saying, 'why don't we meet up for lunch tomorrow? I've a few loose ends to tie up in the office before I leave so I could meet you in that new coffee shop across the road.'

Yes, why not? She could tell him all about tonight's harrowing events, and maybe they'd even have time to brainstorm a few ideas.

She put a hand on his arm. 'I'll see you about one o'clock, if that's all right. I need to call at the hotel for a quick business meeting with Ken, but I can easily be in town by one.'

He nodded, and lapsed into silence. He worked far too hard, Lisa told herself, ignoring her own pounding head. But once they were married, she'd see that he set aside more time for leisure and cut back on the overtime.

His goodnight kiss was pleasant but brief, which was understandable considering how tired he seemed. Things would be different tomorrow when they'd both had a good night's sleep.

★   ★   ★

The next morning Lisa donned her usual T-shirt and jeans, then, catching sight of herself in the mirror, paused to wonder if she'd made the right choice. The day held promise of hot summer sunshine. Why not take the opportunity to wear a dress for a change?

She rummaged in her wardrobe. Yes, there it was. Lurking right at the back amongst her rarely worn, but too-good-to-throw-out category of clothes — a vibrant saffron and orange shift.

Just the thing to wear to her meeting with Ken.

Where had that thought come from? He had no bearing on her choice of clothes — it was Philip who'd prompted her decision.

For the three months they'd known each other, he'd constantly bemoaned the fact that she chose to wear trousers when she wasn't working, rather than dresses. It would be good to show him that the feminine look wasn't beyond her.

Not exactly sure how long the journey to the hotel would take, she opted for an early bus and arrived with quarter of an hour to spare.

She could kill some time by taking a short walk along the seafront, she supposed, but then thought better of it. The high-heeled sandals she'd dug out to complement her dress had begun to rub up a blister. Instead, she went straight to the hotel a little earlier than she'd planned.

The doorman welcomed her. 'If you're looking for the boss, I saw him heading towards the old theatre a few minutes ago. I'd go over and find him if I were you. He's sometimes gone ages over there — goodness knows what he finds to do.'

Lisa hesitated. She didn't want Ken to think she was in any hurry to see him, but . . . her date with Philip . . . ?

'Thanks,' she said, 'I've another meeting to go to after this, so the sooner I get started on this one the better.'

It wasn't until she had walked the full length of the car park, and followed a narrow pathway through a dense clump of bushes and trees, that she could take a proper look at the theatre.

Ken had labelled it an eyesore, and with its boarded-up windows and whitewashed exterior, it would have been easy to dismiss it as such. But to anyone the least bit artistic, it was an architectural gem.

It might have outlived its usefulness as a theatre, but its ornate stone, tiered balcony and delicate carvings made the building worth preserving simply as a piece of art.

But then, Ken wasn't the least bit artistic — his dreadful shirt was proof of that. If only he'd inherited his father's more discerning eye. Perhaps then he'd view both the theatre and Lisa's classes as assets instead of as a couple of embarrassing white elephants.

She'd tell him so as soon as she found him, she resolved, continuing towards the entrance.

The entrance consisted of two solid wooden doors, too stark to be part of the original design but probably far more efficient at keeping out vandals.

One of the doors was bolted, but when Lisa tugged on the second it swung open without so much as a creak. That was a good sign. If the rest of the building had been equally well-maintained, some historical preservation society might be persuaded to take up its case.

Buoyed by the thought, she peered inside. But owing to the boarded-up windows, she couldn't see the state of its upkeep. In fact, she thought, apart from a hotchpotch of trestle tables, folded chairs and large cardboard boxes there was nothing much to be seen at all.

So where was Ken? If he were still in the building, surely she'd hear him moving around. Unless he'd already headed back to the hotel and gone back in through a different entrance.

Yes, if he were here he'd have left a light on. No-one on their right mind would cross the dark foyer with all that clutter to negotiate.

In which case it wouldn't be long before the doorman told him where she was, and he came back to meet her. In the meantime, her blister was becoming more and more painful. She knew she had a plaster in her bag, so she ventured a little farther through the doorway, searching for somewhere to sit. A full-length curtain hung at right angles to the entrance. If it concealed the stairwell leading up to the circle, there was a good chance there would be a light switch somewhere behind it.

She moved forward and let go of the door. Silently it swung closed behind her, plunging the foyer into even deeper gloom. Arms outstretched, she took a step forward and then another. When her fingers closed over the soft velvet of the curtain, she tugged it swiftly aside.

Immediately a shadow leapt out of the stairwell sending her stumbling backwards with a scream. She lost her footing and screamed again when she fell to the floor.

★   ★   ★

In the tiny theatre office, Ken froze, his coffee cup mid-way to his lips. Those screams were coming from here, inside the building. He tutted impatiently — if it turned out to be those two work experience students larking around again, he'd give them very short shrift.

He pulled open the door and reached for the nearest light switch.

However, when the light flashed on, instead of revealing two exuberant teenagers, it showed an ashen-faced Lisa, sprawled on the floor and groaning in pain.

He rushed to her side. 'Lisa, what happened?' He took her gently by the shoulders and eased her into a sitting position.

Her voice was high and shaky, and came out in tight little gasps. 'You tell me . . . I came to meet you . . . and ended up getting . . . attacked!'

'Attacked?' He should call an ambulance. The police, too, if he'd had an intruder. But first he had to find out exactly how badly Lisa was hurt and do his best to calm her.

'Hey, it's all right,' he murmured. 'They won't come back now I'm here

— and if they do, I'll soon see them off.'

'I didn't say it was a person, did I?' she snapped, leaning forward to pull off a shoe and massage the inside of her ankle.

A surge of relief rushed through him. Maybe she'd banged against a table or a rack of folding chairs. This place was little more than a glorified storeroom these days, and a collision with any number of things could have given her a fright.

'There's nothing sinister in here, Lisa,' he said, bending forward to examine her ankle. 'I always check the place when I arrive and again before I leave. Now, can you wiggle your toes?'

She drew a sharp breath and brushed his hand aside. 'And do you check for rats as well? Because that's what jumped out at me.'

'I promise you there are no rats here,' he told her. 'But at the moment I'm more concerned about that ankle — it seems to be giving you a lot of pain.'

Obligingly she wiggled her toes. 'No, it's fine — look. No bruises or swelling, and apart from a small blister, no sign of any damage.' She kicked off the remaining sandal and gave a wry smile. 'Unfortunately I can't say the same about my shoes, but it's a warm dry day, so I suppose there's no reason why I shouldn't go barefoot.'

None whatsoever, except for the small matter of a sprained ankle.

As she levered herself to her feet, taking care not to place all her weight on the suspect foot, he wondered why she wouldn't admit that the ankle was hurting. He had a first aid box in the office and was more than capable of applying a bandage — if she'd let him, which was doubtful.

'Hey, not so fast,' he said, moving forward to help. 'You don't know yet if that ankle will take your weight.'

She shrugged him off. 'My sandal's snapped, not my tendon. So instead of concerning yourself with my non-existent injuries, I suggest you do something about those rats.'

So they were back to the rats again.

'It's gone from singular to plural now, has it?'

She nodded towards the curtain that screened off the stairwell.

'Once I've gone, perhaps you'd like to check behind there. And don't be surprised if you find a whole colony. Pretending the problem doesn't exist isn't going to make it go away.'

He bit back a smile. 'For once could you please trust me? When I said there were no rats in the building, I meant exactly that.'

'But I heard them,' she insisted with a shiver of revulsion. 'And you will too if you stop talking and listen . . . ' She held up her hand. 'There — you must have heard that? It's a squeaking sound, and definitely coming from behind that curtain.'

He strode over to the stairwell. There was only one way to settle this.

'Don't look now,' she yelled, snatching up her shoes. 'If you disturb them they'll be everywhere.'

Would she never trust him?

'Stay very still and don't panic,' he instructed, ignoring her protests. 'And if you can manage to keep that imagination of yours in check for a couple of minutes, I'll do my best to put your mind at rest.'

Up until now, this had been Ken's well-kept secret. He drew the curtain aside and reached for a large cardboard box.

'Scaredy-Cat,' he murmured, setting the box on the floor.

'After what I've just been through,' Lisa hissed, glowering down at him, 'I hardly think it's fair to call me names. Anyone who'd just had a brush with a rat would have reacted in exactly the same way. It was too dark to see and — '

'I wasn't talking about you,' he assured her, crouching over the box and gesturing for her to join him. 'Scaredy-Cat's my nick-name for the nervous little cat who's decided to entrust me with her kittens.'

Lisa's expression changed from horror to fascination.

'Kittens? In there? Oh, let me see.' She knelt at his side, a look of child-like anticipation on her face.

'They're tucked up in one of my old sweaters,' he told her, drawing it gently aside to reveal two tiny black and white kittens. 'They're too young to regulate their own body heat, so I have to keep them warm.'

She gave a gasp of delight. 'Oh ... they're beautiful,' she whispered, 'And so very, very tiny. They can't be more than a couple of weeks old.'

'Getting on for three,' he supplied, with an absurd rush of pride.

'And they've got the most gorgeous blue eyes.' She reached out to stroke them gently, keeping her voice low. 'And such tiny ears — almost flat to their heads.'

'According to the vet, that will alter in another week or so. And they'll be able to purr by then as well.'

'So what's that noise they're making at the moment? I hope they're not frightened. My screams must have given them an awful shock.'

'I think it means they're starting to miss their mum,' he said, pleased to see her smiling again. 'And now that I've managed to convince you I'm not harbouring a colony of rats, it might be a good idea to tuck them up again and put them back where the mother can find them.'

Reluctantly she complied.

'So, where's their mum now?' she asked as he carried the box back behind the curtain.

'I imagine you scared her something rotten when you started screaming. She's probably miles away by now.'

But instead of laughing at his teasing, as he'd expected, she was quiet.

'Lisa?' He backed out of the stairwell and let the curtain fall back.

Her response was a loud sniff, and when he turned to face her he saw that her eyes were brimming with tears.

'Lisa, what is it?' He grimaced. 'It's your ankle, isn't it — I knew it was hurting. Here, let me find you a chair.'

But she shook her head. 'That's why the light wasn't on, isn't it? You wanted to keep them sleeping peacefully together in the dark. And then I came along . . . dragged back the curtain, terrified the mother . . . and screamed so loud she deserted them. It'll be my fault if she doesn't come back and those poor little kittens starve to death,' she sobbed.

He put his arm around her shoulders and pulled her against him. His words had been a joke; a gentle attempt to tease, and he'd expected her to retaliate with a swift come-back.

'Of course they won't starve,' he soothed, brushing back her hair. 'The mother's a cat, not a sparrow, and as soon as everything's quiet, she'll be out from wherever she's hiding.'

'She's left them before?' Lisa asked between sobs.

'Not when they were first born, but

now they don't need feeding quite so often, she sometimes goes off for a short while.'

'But I frightened her, and frightened cats don't always come back. Look at the number that go missing after November the fifth.'

He suppressed a smile. 'Your screams were pretty bloodcurdling, I admit, but I doubt Scaredy-Cat would find them as intimidating as a barrage of fireworks. She's made of sterner stuff than that.'

'You think so?'

'I know so. Now . . . there's another set of stairs on the other side of the entrance. The mother probably shot up there, crossed the circle and is making her way back down to her kittens as we speak.'

She lifted her head and attempted to smile. 'I suppose you think I'm being silly and sentimental?'

He reached for a wayward tendril of her hair, and coiled it around his finger.

'Not at all. It's my own silly

sentimental streak that brings me here three times a day to feed the mother and make sure she's all right.'

When Lisa looked as though she was about to cry again, Ken cupped her face in his hands and bent his head, intending to give her a brief reassuring kiss. But when his lips met hers, he found himself wanting far more than the briefest of kisses. He wanted to pull her into his arms, crush her lips to his, and feel that soft warm body pressed against his chest.

And then he was acting on the impulse. For a long moment she didn't move. Then, as if in slow motion, she arched her body against his, and rose up on tiptoe to curl her arms around his neck.

He tightened his hold and deepened the kiss, his fingers sliding through her tangle of long wavy hair to stroke the soft skin at the nape of her neck. Lisa responded by pressing her body against him and winding her arms more tightly around his neck.

Then, abruptly she jerked back her head and pushed frantically against his shoulders. 'We shouldn't be doing this.'

With a sigh, he disentangled his fingers from her hair and trailed his hands down her arms. For a short while there she'd been a very willing participant. Until she'd remembered the accountant?

'Don't tell me — Philip.'

She bent to scoop up her sandals.

'I'm sorry . . . I don't know what came over me. Philip and I . . . we're practically engaged.'

'What does 'practically engaged' mean? You either are or you aren't.'

'Let's not complicate things, Ken. It's a serious relationship. So for the short time we'll be working together let's keep everything strictly on a business footing, shall we? That way everyone knows where they stand.'

'Suits me,' he told her, wondering why the sudden reminder that they wouldn't be working together for long caused such a stab of regret.

It wasn't as if he'd ever intended her and her classes to be anything more than a temporary distraction. They were a pleasant diversion, that was all. Something to help him through an arduous phase in his life and prevent him getting too bogged down with work.

So what now? She surely wasn't waiting for him to apologise?

She looked up. 'So . . . ' she said, in an infuriatingly remote little voice 'If we're both in agreement, why don't we sit down and discuss business as planned? It is, after all, what I'm here for.'

Her swift change of attitude stunned him. One minute she'd been kissing him with a dizzying lack of restraint and the next she was suggesting that they both calmly sit down and discuss marketing strategies.

Well, he didn't want to. What he wanted was to pull her back into his arms, kiss her senseless and make her forget all about Philip. But from the expression in her eyes, he knew it wasn't going to happen and he'd better let go of the thought pretty quickly.

Here he was, his heart still hammering a mile a minute, and she, not only acting as if the kiss had never happened, but expecting him to join in the charade.

For a long moment neither of them spoke. Then as the seconds passed and both stood awkwardly regarding the other, Ken's irritation began to subside. Maybe her request wasn't so ridiculous after all. Maybe launching into a business discussion would serve as a face-saver and set their relationship back on its original footing.

He made a quick decision. If she could pretend the kiss hadn't happened, then he could too. He wasn't the type of man to split up a happy relationship. But first he had to get her out of here, and into a more public setting. Remaining alone with her offered too many temptations, and he wasn't sure he could trust himself.

'Good idea, but wouldn't you rather go over to the hotel? It'll be more comfortable and I did promise you coffee in the restaurant.'

She looked doubtfully at her bare feet. 'Crossing the car park could be a bit hazardous without any shoes, so I'll pass on that if you don't mind.'

He'd be happy to use his car to ferry her across — anything rather than remain alone with her in this intimate, secluded place.

But crossing the car park wasn't the real problem, he suspected. She'd winced when she'd placed too much weight on that ankle, and he felt sure it was hurting far more than she was letting on. Walking the length of the foyer to get to the restaurant was probably more than she could manage right now.

It would be interesting to know how she intended getting home, though. With no shoes to speak of and a dodgy ankle, she was hardly in any fit state to hop on a bus and she was clearly in far too independent a frame of mind to accept a lift or the offer of a taxi.

Either way it was no business of his. As she'd so carefully pointed out, they were business colleagues, nothing more — and the only person with any cause to be concerned with her welfare was the completely undeserving, 'don't-bother-me' Philip.

Lisa could have her business meeting, if that was what she wanted. They'd pretend the last five minutes had never happened. And while they were debating his strategies for enticing more people to her classes, he'd be wondering what it would take to entice her back into his arms, and if she was equally responsive when she kissed Philip.

She eased herself into the chair, and then looked up, awaiting his answer. Her voice might be cool but her heightened colour and flushed cheeks were sending out conflicting signals.

He gave what he hoped was a nonchalant shrug. 'In that case, I'll make us some coffee. Do you take yours white or black?'

She glanced at her watch. 'I haven't time, I'm afraid. I'm due to meet Philip in town for lunch and need to be out of here in fifteen minutes.'

This girl's optimism knew no bounds. If she thought crossing the hotel car park was hazardous, how on earth did she envisage getting into town? He unfolded a chair and set it down opposite her, being sure to leave a respectable distance between them.

'Right, very quickly, then. This is what I thought we'd try first, if you're in agreement — '

She held up a hand. 'Before you start, I have a favour to ask.'

Ah . . . Miss Independence wasn't as reckless as he'd thought, and was about to ask him to ring for a taxi.

'Go on . . . ' He pulled his mobile from his pocket.

'Since I'm going to be without a car for a week or two, could I leave my sound system and CDs at the hotel after tomorrow's class, so that I'm free to come and go by bus?'

He thrust the mobile back. 'Philip's refused you a lift?'

'Not at all. He'd be happy to help, but unfortunately he's travelling to Manchester later today, and I'll be stuck with public transport for at least the next week.'

Still no mention of a taxi. Maybe she was more deeply in debt than she cared to admit. He regarded her closely.

'And that's how you got here today right?'

Her brows lifted and she gave him a frosty look. 'Your point being?'

This brisk business-like manner didn't suit her. He much preferred the warm, passionate Lisa who'd curled her arms around his neck and kissed him as though she never wanted to stop.

'I wasn't about to make a point,' he said, 'merely to offer you a lift.'

She tilted her chin. 'The bus will be fine, thank you. There's no need for you to put yourself out. Now, getting back to my original question ... Do you have a secure storage place or not?'

Definitely reckless, he thought. Not to mention stubborn, high-handed, and totally infuriating.

'There's a lockable cupboard under the stage,' he said, trying to keep his voice steady. 'You're welcome to keep everything in there.'

Suddenly he wanted to leave. He'd had enough of being calm and business-like, and if he couldn't scoop Lisa into his arms and kiss her until they both longed for breath, then he didn't want to be alone with her any more. He stood and was searching his mind for a diplomatic way to bring the meeting to a close when the door swung open behind him.

* * *

Scaredy-Cat shot in, closely followed by one of the girls from Reception.

'I'm here to remind you about your lunch date,' she said. 'We heard you arranging it this morning and when we saw your car was still in the car park, we thought . . . '

He perched on the edge of a table.

'You thought what, exactly?'

The girl affected a concerned expression. 'We wondered if you'd forgotten the time, and thought one of us ought to come over and remind you.'

Amusement quirked his mouth. They wondered whether his lunch date was centred around business or pleasure, more like, and they'd sent this one over to find out.

'That was very . . . thoughtful of you, but as I didn't specify any particular time, there's no need for anyone to panic just yet.'

A smile tipped the corners of her mouth. 'That seems a bit casual.'

That guileless expression didn't fool him. He'd overheard those girls on Reception discussing their chances of coercing him into a date, and he wasn't about to offer them the slightest encouragement.

'Not at all. It simply means that we're eating at her place, and I've arranged to be there as soon as I can. Like . . . ' he looked pointedly at his watch, 'in the next ten minutes.'

The receptionist nodded, but continued to linger in the doorway.

'So . . . was there anything else?' Ken prompted.

'If you're in a hurry, it doesn't matter. I can call in at your office later. What time do you expect to be back?'

He could have said 'In a couple of hours' and left it at that. But something about her eager expression prompted him to go off on a different tack. The sooner she and the other female employees realised he wasn't up for grabs, the sooner he'd get them off his back.

He assumed a rakish smile. 'It all depends on how things go. The lady's cooking me lunch, so the time I get back will depend on what she has planned for dessert.'

Lisa stood up abruptly and limped to the door.

'Bye, Ken. I have to go.'

He jumped down from the table. 'Hey, not so fast. I'll give you a lift.'

She pulled open the door and stepped through. 'Not necessary,' she called over her shoulder.

'Lisa, wait. You're not wearing any shoes, you can't . . . '

Too late. She'd gone.

He would have followed immediately but he wasn't about to leave the receptionist alone in the building. If she got wind of those kittens it wouldn't be long before the rest of the staff were pestering to see them.

'Right. Come on,' he said, jerking his head towards the door. 'I have to lock up.'

Her face fell, but she did as he asked, albeit at a snail's pace. By the time he'd switched off the lights and locked up, Lisa had almost reached the bus stop.

'Lisa! Wait!' he yelled, striding across the car park.

She ignored him and continued to hobble.

'Lisa!' he roared, causing half a dozen people to whirl round.

Just then a bus rounded the corner and slowed to a halt.

He broke into a sprint, but by the time he reached the stop, the bus had slipped back into the traffic, taking Lisa along with it.

He gazed after it. What, in God's name, had caused her to take off like that? If he hadn't known better he'd have said she was jealous.

A smile crept across his lips at this. The idea wasn't impossible. Maybe he wasn't the only one to have felt more than a spark of attraction. Maybe she wasn't as happy with the wonderful Philip as she made out?

His smile broadened as he climbed into his car. If a fantasy girlfriend was what it took to make Lisa realise she had feelings for him, then maybe he should continue the fantasy?

But to what end? Unless he was

prepared to change his plans for the hotel, which he categorically was not, then any relationship with Lisa was doomed before it had even begun. And what sort of man would he be to entice her away from her steady boyfriend for nothing more than a short-term fling?

He started the car. She wasn't for him, and he should put all such thoughts out of his mind and leave her to marry Philip.

There'd be other women once this one was gone from his life. Equally as pretty, just as lively — and if he chose carefully, without the complication of a serious boyfriend.

But would they be as intriguing as this one? And so wickedly exciting to kiss?

Oh Dear, Lisa!

The bus was full of holidaymakers so, to Lisa's relief, her bare feet didn't seem out of place among the assortment of skimpy clothes and attracted only fleeting glances.

But when the bus dropped her in the centre of town half an hour later, the glances changed to puzzled stares. Perhaps it would help if she hid her shoes in her bag, she thought, moving to the inside of the pavement.

As she paused to organise it, she found herself outside the smart new coffee shop where she'd arranged to meet Philip. Now all she had to do was find him.

She glanced through the window to see if he was already inside, only to discover she was being scrutinised by a group of elaborately coiffured middle-aged women.

She resisted the urge to poke out her tongue and returned her attention to the shop's interior. It was a bar, coffee shop and art gallery all rolled into one, with the décor enhanced by dozens of colourful paintings. Stylish without being formal.

So why the snooty looks? Lisa closed her bag, sent the cement hair-dos an 'I've-as-much-right-to-be-here-as-you-do' glare, and stepped boldly into the building.

Too late, she remembered her injured ankle. As she stepped over the threshold, her grand entrance collapsed in an ungainly stumble, prompting a buzz of disparaging comments from her audience.

Lisa sent them a challenging look. The ringleader, a svelte woman with austere blue-black hair swept into an elegant chignon, immediately gripped the arm of her nearest companion.

'I do hope this place isn't going to attract too many bohemian types,' she said more loudly than necessary. 'It would really lower the tone.'

A hum of agreement followed. Lisa ignored them.

As there was no sign of Philip at any of the tables, she headed for the ladies' cloakroom. Perhaps she could find a way of fixing her sandal before he arrived. In light of the comments she'd attracted, she'd better try, even if the repair only lasted while she ate her lunch.

'I hope she's not going in there to smoke anything illegal,' came the piercing tones of the Elegant Chignon. 'Perhaps I ought to ask one of the waitresses to keep an eye on her.'

Lisa continued across the room, her eyes fixed straight ahead. The women were showing themselves up, not her. Genuinely well-bred people wouldn't dream of passing such spiteful remarks, especially ones that were so obviously untrue. Apart from the small matter of her lack of shoes, Lisa had respectability written all over her.

Or so she'd happily believed. One

glance in the cloakroom mirror and that illusion evaporated. She stared at her reflection in horror. The face that stared back at her was not only blotchy and tear-stained, but also sported the odd streak of dust and grime. To cap it all, her hair hung in an untidy tangle with tiny clumps of cobwebs clinging to the ends. What a dreadful sight she was!

She grabbed a paper towel and turned on the tap. Thank goodness she'd come in here before Philip arrived! He'd probably have taken one look at her and insisted they ate sandwiches in the park.

Five minutes of dabbing and scrubbing and she began to breathe more easily. It would only another minute to apply her make-up and tug a brush through her hair, and she'd be presentable again.

That done, she slapped a plaster on her blister, and used a couple more to carry out a makeshift repair to the strap of her sandal. It wouldn't hold after she'd left the coffee shop, of course, but with any luck, if she remained seated throughout the meal, nobody would be any the wiser.

Once she explained the situation to Philip, he was sure to drive her home, even if it meant him being a bit late setting off on his journey.

She really was lucky to have such a solid and dependable boyfriend, she thought with a fond smile. Ken Huntley might be good looking and charming, but those qualities came at a price. One girlfriend would never be enough for a man like him. He seemed to have a compulsion to hone that charm on every female he met, and flirting was all part of the game. He could never offer the safe and secure type of relationship she shared with Philip. It would go completely against the grain.

She only hoped the hapless female he was meeting for lunch was aware of the man's fickle tendencies. How awful it would be to fall for somebody like him and then discover you were only one of many.

One last glance in the mirror confirmed that she was ready to face the world on equal terms, and despite the dull throbbing in her ankle, she stepped back into the coffee shop with a regal air.

She was just in time to see Philip pull out a chair at the table next to the cement hair-dos.

No, Philip — not there!

She called his name and tried to indicate that she'd rather sit somewhere else, but he simply smiled and beckoned her over.

By the time she'd made her way across, he was settled in his seat and making small-talk with the women.

'Philip,' she butted in, deliberately ignoring the group. 'Do you think we could — ?'

'Yes, of course, but first I'd like you to meet my mother.'

His mother? Who? Where?

The Elegant Chignon stood up, a serene smile plastered across her face.

'So, you're Lisa,' she said, the smile

changing to a smirk. 'I'm about to leave so we'll have to become acquainted some other time, I'm afraid.'

Sometime never, her eyes said, as she continued to smile.

'Enjoy your meal. It's quite an experience eating here. You see a completely different side of life.'

Philip regarded her in some puzzlement. 'It's a surprise to find you here. It's not one of your regular lunch spots.'

She placed a hand on his arm. 'No, dear, but I thought I ought to give it a go, considering they're one of your clients.'

'You don't find it a little . . . unsophisticated?'

She stared directly at Lisa. 'I find unsophisticated places quite amusing. Like unsophisticated people — brash, but amusing.'

Lisa felt a flush rise up her neck and spread across her face. This was dangerous ground. One word out of turn and she'd not only alienate Philip's mother for ever, but cause Philip untold embarrassment.

With supreme effort she stood mutely at his side, her hands clenched so tightly that her nails cut into her palms.

'Isn't she a card?' Philip murmured as his mother led her entourage out through the door. 'I'd noticed myself that the paintings seemed a little on the bright side, but it took my mother's apt turn of phrase to make me realise how hideously gaudy they really are.'

Lisa took a deep, calming breath and sat down. Could Philip's mother have been talking about the paintings? It was feasible, she supposed, but from the way the woman had narrowed her gaze to focus solely on Lisa, she very much doubted it.

Philip passed her a menu. 'You have a look at that while I tell you my news. Things are really starting to look up career-wise.'

For *his* career, maybe, Lisa thought. But her own was quite a different story.

'Lisa? Are you listening?'

She looked up, her face still burning with humiliation. 'Yes, go on.'

His expression was one of suppressed excitement. 'The senior partner called me in this morning and made it quite clear that if I continue to work at my present rate for the next two or three years, I'll be in the running for a partnership myself.'

Despite her bad morning, Lisa managed to summon a smile. 'That's great, Philip. It sounds as though they've made the decision already.'

'Yes, I'd come to that conclusion myself.' He gave a satisfied sigh. 'Do you realise I'll be the youngest partner the firm's ever had? That's no mean feat when you consider the size of it.'

'I'm pleased for you. I only wish my own career was going as well.'

That was his cue to pitch in and help her brainstorm a few ideas. But the conversation remained fixed on his own hopes and ambitions all through the meal.

'Goodness, look at the time,' he said when he returned from settling the bill. 'I should be on the road by now.'

'I don't suppose you could run me home, could you?' Lisa asked. 'I twisted my ankle on the way here and it's starting to stiffen up.'

He looked down at her outstretched foot. 'I can't see any swelling. You've probably got off lightly. But why's that scruffy piece of plaster stuck to your shoe? It doesn't look very fetching.'

She tensed. 'I don't imagine it does, but since I also snapped the strap on my sandal, the choice was make-do-and-mend or go barefoot.'

He gave her a despairing look. 'If you'd only take life at a more ladylike pace you wouldn't get yourself into these predicaments.'

He sat down again and took his phone out of his pocket. 'I haven't time to drive you home but I'll order you a taxi.'

She slumped back in her chair. That would cost her a pretty packet, but the discomfort in her ankle ruled out another trip on the bus.

'It'll be about ten minutes,' he said. 'Why don't you have another coffee while you're waiting? And if you move into that seat my mother had by the window, you'll be able to see your taxi as soon as it pulls up.'

Ah yes — his mother.

'Philip — about your mother . . . '

He smiled. 'Wasn't it a stroke of luck us bumping into her here? She's been wanting to meet you.'

She tried to look suitably enthusiastic. 'Wasn't it? The thing is, when I fell, I was looking for Ken in a derelict storeroom and ended up covered in dust and cobwebs. So I was looking a bit the worse for wear . . . '

'She won't hold that against you. I told her you're a bit of a tomboy.'

'Even so, I'd like you to explain to her that I don't normally go around looking quite so unkempt.'

He studied her for a moment and nodded. 'With your type of hair I imagine the unkempt look is something you're constantly fighting.'

'That's right,' she admitted, pleased that he understood. 'Usually when I least want it to happen.'

He gave her an affectionate smile. 'That's what I thought, and I can't help wondering if now might be an appropriate time to adopt a more elegant image.'

She frowned. 'Go on . . . '

He reached across the table and took her hands in his. 'Something more in keeping with the wife of an up and coming accountant perhaps?'

She was stunned into silence. What had he just said? She blinked.

'Was that a proposal?' she asked slowly.

'What do you think?'

She didn't know what to think. One moment he seemed to be criticising her and the next he was talking about marriage.

'Lisa?'

Wasn't he supposed to tell her he loved her? That he couldn't imagine life without her? Wasn't he supposed to hold her and kiss her and make the moment so special that she'd remember it as long as she lived?

But Philip wasn't like that. He was dignified and reserved and would no more dream of revealing his emotions in a public place than he would run naked along the beach. Yet this was still a heartfelt proposal, however clumsily packaged, and if anything that hint of clumsiness made it all the more endearing.

'I think it probably was,' she said quietly.

'I know why you're hesitating. But there's no need — with a bit of coaching, we'll soon have you preparing sumptuous dinner parties and playing the accomplished hostess. There's no need to feel overawed.'

She felt herself tense. 'We?'

'Who better to help you than my

mother? I'm sure that once she gets to know you, she'll be delighted to take you under her wing.'

The proposal suddenly lost its lustre.

'Can we talk about this some other time? My ankle's throbbing, and all I can think about right now is getting home and putting my feet up.'

His face creased into a frown. 'That wasn't the response I expected.'

'I'm sorry,' she said miserably, 'but I don't think I'm in a fit state at the moment to make any life-changing decisions.'

He stood up. 'In that case, I apologise for adding even more stress to your day. I was under the mistaken impression that my proposal might brighten it.'

'And it would have, but . . . '

He held up his hand to silence her. 'No need to explain. I understand perfectly. You go home and have a good rest.'

'Philip, I didn't mean — '

But he was already on his way out of the door. 'Goodbye, Lisa,' he called over his shoulder. 'I'll ring you later — if I have time.'

She closed her eyes. What was the matter with her? If anyone had told her a week ago that Philip was about to propose, she would have been ecstatic.

Mixed Emotions

By seven o'clock he hadn't rung. And can you blame him? Lisa thought, picking up the remote control and flicking on the TV. Philip had sprung a proposal on her, hoping to make her day, and she'd reacted with a complete lack of diplomacy. How could she have behaved that way?

Now that she was better rested and able to think more clearly, she could understand how humiliated the poor man must have felt. She'd be lucky if he ever wanted to see her again.

She could try calling him, of course, but if he still happened to be working it would restrict what she could say, and she could end up making the situation even worse. No, it would be best to wait for him to ring her — even if it meant waiting until ten or eleven o'clock.

In the meantime she needed to eat.

She took a few tentative steps towards the kitchen. Her ankle was still sore, but she seemed to be walking on it more easily. The rest and the cold compress she'd applied must have done it good, she thought, pulling open the fridge door.

Hmmm. Not a lot to tempt her in there — just a solitary carton of yoghurt and a bottle of milk.

A takeaway would have been the best option, she thought, taking the yoghurt and hobbling back to the settee. Unfortunately, the taxi fare had left such a large dent in her money that it was out of the question.

Her funds would run to a loaf of bread and a packet of bacon, though. Maybe she'd manage to walk to the corner shop? But what if Philip were to ring while she was out? She couldn't risk upsetting him again when their relationship was on such a tenuous footing.

She opened the yoghurt. If Philip rang early she'd make the trip to the shop. If not, then she'd wait until morning — it wouldn't kill her to go hungry for one evening.

* * *

By nine o'clock, when Philip still hadn't made contact, Lisa was fighting tantalising images of crisply-cooked bacon.

Her heart lifted when the doorbell chimed. Philip! He'd driven back from Manchester to sort things out! She'd known he couldn't stay angry for long.

She tossed the yoghurt pot in the direction of the bin, muted the TV and hobbled as fast as her ankle would allow to let him in.

'You!'

Ken Huntley stood on the threshold, dressed in jeans and trainers and a remarkably tasteful casual shirt.

'I'm afraid so. Is that a problem?'

'I thought you were Philip.'

He seemed unperturbed. 'In that case, it's time for an eye test.'

'I hoped you were Philip, I meant.'

He shook his head. 'Oh, dear, I can see your mother never taught you the correct way to greet a guest. Now repeat after me. 'Hello, Ken. How nice of you to call. Won't you please come in?' '

'Hello, Ken,' she echoed woodenly. 'What do you want? I'm busy.'

'I've come to check on the state of your ankle, seeing as the fall was partly my fault.'

'Partly?'

He leant against the doorpost. 'All right — wholly.'

She looked down and wiggled her toes. 'It hasn't seized up, if that's what you were hoping — so I won't be cancelling any classes.'

'I didn't image you would.' He grinned. 'Only a full body brace and traction would keep you out of action. You're the most determined person I know.'

'I'm pleased you realise it. Now, if there was nothing else?'

'Well, there is, actually. I promised a

few strategies to increase your student numbers. If we put off the discussion, you could miss out.'

She couldn't argue with that. But did the discussion have to take place this very minute? She'd feel far more comfortable holding it in his office before tomorrow's class. Her small flat seemed too intimate a setting for an impersonal business discussion.

'This isn't a good time.'

His grin widened. 'I haven't come empty-handed.' He reached down and picked up a large plastic carrier. 'How does pizza grab you?' He rummaged among the contents. 'With extra toppings and a generous helping of home-made coleslaw.'

She'd been about to tell him to go away . . .

'Not to mention deep fried potato skins and breaded mushrooms.'

But now she was truly torn . . .

His face fell. 'Don't tell me — you had a late meal and you can't possibly manage another mouthful?'

All she had to do was agree.

He lifted a lid on one of the boxes and the rich smell of cheese and tomatoes pervaded the air. 'There's pepperoni, or if you prefer — '

'Come on in and I'll find us some plates.'

He didn't need telling twice. 'That's what I was hoping you'd say,' he answered, following her into the living-room. 'It takes a strong person to resist one of Franco's carry-outs.'

As long as he realised that was the only reason she was letting him in.

'You caught me at a weak moment — I was too tired to cook and had begun to fantasise about bacon sandwiches.'

He strode over to the coffee table and began unpacking his box.

'If you think bacon sandwiches are living in the fast lane, wait until you try these incredible toppings.'

Lisa sniffed the air. It was months since she'd had a pizza and these smelled absolutely wonderful. This wasn't the first time Ken had lightened her mood with exactly the right gesture, and she couldn't help feeling inordinately pleased.

He looked up and caught her smiling at him. 'Surely I'm not the cause of that delighted expression? I didn't realise my presence was so intoxicating.

'You wish,' she said sweetly, and continued into the kitchen for plates.

Seeing her yoghurt pot perched on the top of the overflowing bin, Ken smiled. 'Is that all you've had? Yoghurt? No wonder you're fantasising about hot food.'

'Talking of hot food,' she said, determined to see him equally rattled, 'how was your hot dessert?'

His grin broadened. 'How nice of you to ask. It turned out to be apple pie, as it happened — one of my all-time favourites.'

'That must have been a disappointment. Weren't you expecting something a little more . . . novel?'

He gave a laugh. 'You ask way too

many questions. Now, are you ready to start our meeting?'

Oh, yes, the meeting. Lisa grabbed two plates and returned to the living-room.

'You mentioned something about these ideas of yours not costing me anything. That sounds a little far-fetched.'

He chuckled, a low, sexy sound that for some reason made her heart do a funny little jig.

'Not for a man with my contacts.'

'I like the sound of this,' she said, handing him a plate. 'Do go on.'

'Well, a week or two ago, the local paper rang to ask if I'd agree to be featured in one of a series of articles they're running on people and their jobs.' He paused to take the lid off the coleslaw. 'I asked them to come back later in the year when my refurbish-ments would be finished and the publicity would do me more good.'

That figured, she thought, flopping down on to the settee. Ken wasn't the sort to do any favours unless there was something in it for him.

'So how does the offer affect me when it's you they want?'

He shot her a sideways glance. 'What if I were to call them back and suggest they do a feature on you? Your job's quirky enough to appeal, and you'd get free publicity. What do you say?'

Not only free, she decided, but probably also a lot more effective than the run-of-the-mill press advertisements she'd previously run.

'I say 'yes,' of course! When do you think they'll be able to come?'

He sat down beside her. 'Pretty soon, I imagine. Have you any preference?'

'The sooner the better, as far as I'm concerned.' She placed one of the plates in front of him and cleared a space for her own. 'Those classes at the leisure centre are due to start next week.'

He tipped his head to one side and regarded her with a smile. 'In that case you shouldn't be too angry when I tell you that I've already called the editor, and he'll be sending a photographer and reporter to Friday night's class.'

Without another thought she squealed and launched herself at him to fling her arms around his neck.

'Of course I'm not angry,' she murmured, her cheek pressed tightly against his. 'It's an absolutely brilliant id — '

His mouth cut off the rest of the sentence, and the next moment she found herself returning his kiss with a passion she hadn't realised she possessed. Why didn't Philip's kisses provoke such a response in her, she wondered, revelling in the warmth of Ken's body. It was so unfair that she should feel such head-spinning, spine-tingling elation kissing a man she had no feelings for . . .

Philip! What was she doing? She pulled away and abruptly sat up.

'A simple 'thank you' would have done,' Ken said. 'But I'm not complaining. Can I expect a similar response when you hear business idea number two?'

Stay calm, Lisa told herself. This is only as embarrassing as you allow it to be. Make light of it and he'll let the matter drop.

'There are more?' She leant over the table to prevent him from seeing the flush on her face and gave careful attention to her portion of pizza.

He followed suit, his shoulder resting against hers.

'But of course. Unless you have any ideas of your own that you want to run past me?'

She took a deep, steadying breath.

'Not really. I'd hoped to brainstorm a few with Philip but he had more pressing matters on his mind.'

'Now why doesn't that surprise me?'

He filled his plate then leant back, leaving her suddenly chilled.

'I wasn't criticising him — just stating a fact.' She paused to take a bite of pizza. 'I think it's good that he's so involved in his work. Not many men his age are so conscientious and reliable.'

'For conscientious and reliable, read dull. Let's face it, Lisa — the man's old before his time. He can't be more than twenty-two or three; at that age he should be out having fun. I've seen livelier octogenarians.'

She looked at him sharply. 'Not every woman wants a fun-loving charmer. Especially when that charm brings nothing but misery.'

He leant forward to brush a strand of hair from her face.

'So, who was this charmer, Lisa? He must have made a pretty big impact on your life to make you so determined to settle for a man like Philip.'

She debated whether or not to tell him.

'It's all right,' he said, his voice soft and low. 'I understand if you don't want to talk about it.'

She suddenly had the crazy urge to curl into his side, to lean her head on his chest and tell him everything. She knew better than to act on it, but the thought of snuggling against him did nothing to help her composure.

She turned her face away, and dragged in a deep breath.

'It was my father . . . You say your mother was hardly ever around? Well, my father was around even less. He left home when I was five years old and only came back intermittently after that . . .'

Her words fell into silence. An easy, companionable silence that she felt no immediate urge to fill.

Ken set his plate aside and leaned back into the cushions. When Lisa looked up he was watching her with a strangely intense expression.

'By the sound of things, he left quite a few scars,' he said gently.

'Too right.' She struggled to force the words out past the lump in her throat. 'I've lost count of the number of promises he made and broke over the years. I'd be waiting for him to come and pick me up for some special outing, only to have him not turn up

— without any explanation.'

He touched her cheek. 'Go on . . . ' he urged, the tenderness of the gesture causing her eyes to fill with tears.

She swallowed. 'My mother told him to stay away at one point, thinking it would be for the best, but I missed him so much she was forced to reconsider. In spite of his infrequent visits and broken promises, he was so affectionate when he finally did come to see me that I was totally devoted to him.'

'So, where did he go when he left? Was there another woman?'

'Plenty, I imagine. He sang with a jazz band and would go on the road for weeks at a time. They weren't house-hold names or anything like that, but they made a comfortable living.'

'And did your mother ever see any of that money?'

'At first. Then he disappeared abroad without leaving a forwarding address. My mother became so short of money that she opened up a dance school and took me along with her each evening to save on babysitting costs.'

'And you've never heard from him since?'

'I saw him once when I was about thirteen years old, when I was waiting for some friends in the shopping precinct. He had another family by then, and judging by the expression on the faces of the two little girls clutching his hands, they worshipped him as much as I had. I didn't speak to him, and I doubt whether he'd have recognised me if I had.'

She squeezed her eyes shut to force back the tears. 'So, you see I've had it with charmers. I want a husband who's solid and dependable — someone I know I can rely on.'

'And you think you've found that with Philip?'

'I know I have. He's not the flighty type and never will be. He's open and honest and, apart from today, he's never done anything to upset me.'

'So what happened today?' Ken asked softly.

'We had a bit of a tiff, that's all, but nothing that can't be fixed.'

'That's if you want to fix it, of course.'

She stared at him. 'Of course I want to. Why wouldn't I?'

He gave a small, humourless laugh.

'A few moments ago you practically hurled yourself into my lap. What does that say about your feelings for Philip?'

'This may come as a bit of a shock to you,' she snapped, struggling to hold back her temper, 'but I gave you a grateful hug, that was all. And only someone with your massive ego could have failed to recognise that.'

He placed his hands behind his head in an infuriatingly relaxed pose.

'If that's what you want to believe, then fine, go ahead. But ask yourself this: do you really want to spend your life with that boring windbag when there are far more suitable men out there?'

'Philip is not boring. He's intelligent, and knowledgeable, and . . . '

'Mind-numbingly dull.'

That was so unfair.

'What you're saying is that because he hasn't your craving for the limelight he's got no personality? Well, I'd rather have someone like him than an attention-seeking womaniser like you.'

He stared at her in silence.

'Is that really how you see me?' he asked at last.

'Yes, if today was anything to go by. You were kissing me in the morning, flirting with your receptionist shortly after, and romancing the Hot Pudding Queen over lunch. Hardly the behaviour of a one-woman man, is it?'

'Lisa, that's so not true . . . '

'Is it? I — ' A trill from the telephone cut off the rest of her answer.

'Leave it,' Ken ordered. 'We need to sort this out.'

She ignored him and hobbled to the phone.

'Lisa, I'm sorry,' came Philip's fraught voice. 'Issuing you with an ultimatum was extremely unfair. Take all the time you need.'

'The answer's yes,' she said at once.

There was a stunned silence at the other end of the phone.

'Philip, I said yes,' she repeated, and she turned so that her eyes locked with Ken's. 'I'll be delighted to marry you.'

He heaved a sigh of relief. 'That's that little problem sorted out then. Why you couldn't have said as much this morning instead of keeping me on tenterhooks all day, I really don't know.'

She searched Ken's expression for some indication of dismay, but saw only indifference.

'We'll have a long talk about it when you get back,' she said, schooling her features into an elated smile. 'But all that matters for now is the fact that we're going to be married — just as soon as it can be arranged.'

At that, Ken came over to her side, placed a hand over the mouthpiece and whispered, 'Goodnight — I'll see myself out.'

And that was that. No attempts to

talk her out of it, just a quiet and unobtrusive exit.

Which is exactly what Lisa had wanted, of course.

Saying goodbye to Philip, she picked up the empty pizza boxes and ripped them to shreds. Maybe now Ken would keep well away from her, and seek his romantic challenges somewhere else.

★ ★ ★

When Lisa arrived at the hotel the next afternoon, her wish seemed to have been granted. Ken's car wasn't parked in its usual place and she couldn't see it anywhere else.

'Don't worry,' the taxi driver told her. 'If you're looking for someone to carry your stuff in for you, I can spare you a couple of minutes.'

She thanked him and led the way into the ballroom.

One or two dancers had already arrived, but Ken was nowhere around. Lisa instructed the taxi driver to leave her sound system at the edge of the stage, then offered him a drink for his trouble.

He declined with a smile. 'All part of the service.'

She watched him go. She'd been led to believe that a DJ was part of the hotel service, she thought, so why wasn't Ken here, and more to the point, did he intend turning up at all?

'Excuse me, Lisa . . . ' Lisa turned to see Yvette split from a group seated at one of the tables by the stage. 'If you're looking for Ken, you've just missed him. He called in about ten minutes ago and asked me to give you this.' She held out a key. 'He said to tell you it's for the cupboard under the stage, and he's sorry he can't be here to give it to you himself, but he has some urgent business to sort out.'

Lisa bet he had. 'Did he say when he'd be back?'

Yvette shook her head. 'He was in such a hurry, he hardly had time to say much at all. He just left me the key and rushed off.'

He'd done it deliberately, Lisa thought, taking the key and tucking it into the pocket of her jeans. Unable to accept that any woman in her right mind would choose a life of stability over a casual fling, he'd gone off in a fit of the sulks.

Well, let him. And if, from now on, he found a pressing appointment to coincide with every one of her classes, that was fine by her. She hadn't wanted a DJ in the first place and could manage perfectly well without one. His absence was a cause for celebration rather than anything else.

'I expect it was something unavoidable,' Yvette went on. 'I'm sure he wouldn't intentionally let anyone down.'

Sulking or not, Ken had obviously managed to charm Yvette. Two days ago she'd had no qualms about putting him in his place and now here she was, positively sticking up for him.

Lisa resisted the urge to disagree. It

was unprofessional and would make the situation awkward if Ken returned before the end of the class.

'Don't worry, Yvette. I'm used to working by myself. I'm sure Ken realised I'd be able to cope.'

And cope she did — after a fashion. But the stage at the hotel was far bigger than the one she'd been used to at the town hall, and it wasn't long before the constant hopping between sound system and dance floor began to take its toll on her injured ankle.

Perhaps she'd been a bit hasty in hoping Ken wouldn't come back, she conceded after a particularly energetic number. Despite the support of her sturdy lace-up boots, her ankle was beginning to throb. She badly needed time out to rest it.

She solved the problem temporarily by bringing the interval forward, but that meant she now had the longest part of the session to come. How was she going to last out?

'Is there anything I can do to help?'

Yvette asked as Lisa sat down beside her. 'All that dashing about must be wearing you out.'

Lisa tried to look cheerful. 'Not unless you fancy a stint as a DJ. I didn't realise things would be quite so hectic without Ken.'

'Seriously?' Yvette's face lit up. 'Would you really let me?'

Lisa hadn't the heart to tell her that the invitation had been a joke, nothing more than a thinly-disguised dig at Ken. But since Yvette seemed so pleased that she'd offered, why not take her up on it?

'If you think you can do it,' she said with an answering smile, 'then I'd be delighted to show you the ropes. It's frantic up there on my own.'

Yvette smacked her glass down and jumped to her feet. 'I'm always open to a new challenge. Let's get this show on the road.'

Within fifteen minutes, Yvette had proved herself a keen and efficient worker. And if she was occasionally overcome by the urge to pick up the microphone and add a few snappy comments of her own, Lisa could live with that. At least she wasn't sporting a tasteless shirt or repeatedly absconding to mingle with the audience.

For the hundredth time that afternoon, Lisa looked towards the door. If Ken did return before the end of the class, she didn't want to miss the expression on his face when he found they were managing without him.

But as the afternoon wore on it looked as though that pleasure was to be denied her. No matter — she'd coped without causing her ankle too much strain, and that was the main thing.

'Thank you very much, Yvette,' Lisa said, when the class came to an end..'I don't know how I'd have managed without you.'

Yvette lifted the last CD out of the machine and switched the power off.

'Any time, my dear. I can't tell you how important it makes me feel being entrusted with such an impressive piece of equipment.'

'It's that, all right,' Lisa said with a sigh. 'And unless I get my student numbers up, it's going to be a struggle to pay for it.'

'What you need is a run of free publicity,' Yvette said earnestly.

'The local paper is sending a photographer and a reporter to tomorrow night's class.' Lisa told her with a grin. 'Maybe that'll do the trick.'

Yvette beamed at her. 'I'm sure it will. I might treat myself to a shirt and a pair of jeans. It would be nice to look the part for the photos.'

Lisa was about to explain that the idea was Ken's, when someone called across the hall.

'Don't forget you're giving us a lift, Yvette!'

'Coming!' Yvette replied. 'Can I offer you a lift too, Lisa? I live in Radcliff, but I could drop you in almost any part of Sandford.'

'I live near St Aidan's Church, if that's not too far out of your way.'

'No problem at all. We'll wait for you in the car park.'

What a lovely person, Lisa thought. Why couldn't Philip's mother be more like her?

Yvette's car had a sumptuous interior and as the other women chatted, Lisa allowed herself the luxury of sinking into the plush upholstery and gazing idly out of the window.

But it wasn't long before she was jolted out of her complacency by the sight of Ken's distinctive blue car parked outside a row of shops on a little road leading down to the promenade. Seated on the forecourt of one of those shops, relaxing under a huge parasol, was Ken himself . . . accompanied by a stunning redhead.

Lisa closed her eyes. He hadn't been to any business meeting. He'd simply fancied an afternoon off — and while she'd been running herself ragged struggling to do two jobs at once, he'd been enjoying a tranquil afternoon in the sun with one of his girlfriends!

A First Class Dance Class

Lisa spent a restless night, but to her relief, the constant clambering on and off stage hadn't caused any lasting damage to her ankle. Apart from a little stiffness, she was able to move about as normal.

Just to be on the safe side, however, she put her feet up at every opportunity, which was how she came to be spending the early part of the evening watching the regional TV news.

One of Radcliff's biggest clothing stores was closing down, ending its days with a massive sale. In a series of quick, on-the-spot interviews, individual shoppers were being asked to share details of their bargains. Hardly riveting stuff. Lisa was about to get up and make a sandwich, when who should appear on the screen but Yvette?

'I was lucky enough to get these

jeans,' she told the interviewer, holding two or three pairs up for the camera. 'And four beautiful shirts as well. I've bought them to wear to these amazing line-dance classes I've just joined at the Cliff Hotel in Sandford. They're held three times a week and are the most incredible fun.'

'You dance three times a week? No wonder you look so trim.' The interviewer made to move on, but Yvette snatched the microphone from him. 'It's the best exercise going. And if anyone would like to join us, the class is at seven-thirty to ten-thirty, Tuesdays and Fridays and Thursday afternoons from two until four.'

Lisa punched the air. Never in her wildest dreams had she imagined getting a plug like that. Yvette was an absolute marvel.

Too excited to give food more than a passing thought, she danced from the living-room into her bedroom where she hauled an eye-catching red camisole out of her wardrobe. Yvette's mention was an omen, she thought, fingering the rich embroidery and fringed hem — a sign that things were finally going right for her. And when hordes of new students arrived at her class tonight, she wanted to be wearing something glitzy to greet them.

The outfit certainly had an impact on Ken. 'That fringy thing's very nice,' he said the minute she stepped into the ballroom. 'I wonder if they do a matching one for men?'

'Don't even think about it,' she said, squashing on her Stetson. 'And don't think you can get round me with flattery, either. I want to know where you were yesterday afternoon and why you let me down.'

'I had a meeting.'

He'd have to do better than that.

'Can I ask who with?' She smiled sweetly.

'You can.'

'So — who was it with?'

'I said you could ask — I didn't say I would tell you.'

He wasn't even sorry, she thought furiously.

'Because that might incriminate you, I suppose?'

He grinned. 'Because if you knew everything about me, it would spoil the mystery. Now why don't you let me buy you a drink by way of apology? There's a good few minutes yet before we need start the class.'

He made a move towards the bar.

'You don't get off that easily,' she said, pulling him back. 'I'll have you know that while you were sharing a leisurely picnic with the Hot Pudding Queen, I was struggling to do two jobs at once — to the detriment of my sore ankle.'

He looked truly sorry. 'I give you my word, Lisa, that the meeting was business, very last minute, and that neither a picnic nor the Hot Pudding Queen were in any way involved.'

He wasn't going to come clean, that was for sure, so she supposed she would have to let the matter drop.

'In that case, lead on to the bar — I want to talk to you about Yvette.'

He suddenly looked very wary.

'Come on,' she said. 'I know you find her exasperating at times, but the woman's an absolute treasure. You wouldn't believe what she did for me today . . . '

His face relaxed. 'Go on, surprise me.'

He didn't look very surprised when she told him. Amused maybe, but not surprised.

'So I suppose you want me to be extra nice to her now?' he said.

'It's not a lot to ask.'

'Even when she pushes her nose into things that don't concern her?'

'Especially then, because that's when she's standing up for me, and heaven knows I can do with the support.'

'You've certainly picked the right person to champion your cause,' he murmured. 'What's the betting she was a double-glazing salesman in a previous existence?'

That wasn't fair.

'Have you ever stopped to think,' she said, giving him a stern look, 'that the reason you find her so irritating is that the two of you are so much alike? If it wasn't for the age difference, it would be a definite case of separated at birth. So think about that next time you're tempted to criticise her.'

His face was a picture. It changed from amusement to shock, then disbelief, finally settling back to amusement again when Lisa gave in to the urge to laugh.

'Very droll,' he said. 'But now that you've made your point, can we talk about something else? All this amateur psychology is making me quite uncomfortable.'

Lisa smirked; it was all right for him to compare Yvette to a salesman, but he didn't like being lumped in the same category himself. He probably thought of himself as a something with a much fancier title, such as 'promoter' or 'entrepreneur'.

'Point taken,' she said, beginning to recover her composure. 'What would you like to talk about?'

After Wednesday evening's turn of events, she was expecting the conversation to go directly to Philip. But Ken had either forgotten all about Philip's phone call, or simply couldn't care less, because he made absolutely no reference to it. The next few minutes were spent discussing her play list and then he suggested they return to the ballroom.

For some reason, this left Lisa feeling vaguely disappointed. She didn't have time to dwell on the matter, though, because the room was rapidly filling up and she had more pressing concerns to claim her attention — such as counting the number of new faces, and finding Yvette to thank her.

The latter proved to be the more difficult, and after repeatedly skimming the room, Lisa was forced to conclude that despite Yvette's keen enthusiasm, she wasn't among tonight's crowd.

It wasn't until she saw Ken waving to an elegant figure in a white Stetson that she realised Yvette had been there all along — she just hadn't recognised her in her new clothes.

Lisa immediately issued a public and heartfelt thank you, earning Yvette a spontaneous round of applause. Even Ken joined in, Lisa was pleased to note. It was good to see him making the effort to be more friendly towards her, especially when Yvette was so ready to stick up for him.

'She must have spent a small fortune on all that gear,' Ken muttered as they brought the first half of the session to a close. 'Perhaps someone should remind her that the class is only here on a temporary basis.'

'And perhaps somebody should remind you that I intend this class to run and run,' Lisa said sweetly. 'So your concerns are completely unnecessary.'

'You've found somewhere then? Why didn't you tell me?'

'No, I haven't, as you well know. But

for someone who promised to do his best to help me find another place, I don't hear you coming up with many suggestions.'

His expression sobered. 'You're right, and what can I say? I've neglected to keep my side of the bargain. But I promise you that's about to change.' His mouth curved into a smile. 'And with two of us looking, it shouldn't be too difficult.'

Only one of us, actually, Lisa thought, as she followed him down from the stage. She wanted the Cliff Hotel and nothing else would do, so why should she bother wasting her time searching for something that didn't exist?

★   ★   ★

The first half of the session went well, but as Lisa kicked off the second by throwing herself into yet another lively dance routine, Ken couldn't help wondering if she wasn't pushing herself

184

a little too hard. His mother's TV debut had resulted in a significant increase in numbers, and he could understand Lisa wanting to make sure that the class lived up to the hype. But if she didn't take it easy on that ankle, he could see her coming a cropper at any moment.

'What do you think you're doing?' she demanded when he announced that the next dance would be a leisurely rumba. 'That's not on my play list. What happened to 'Walk the Line'?'

'I don't want your ankle taking too much of a battering, so I'm giving you the chance to ease up.'

'I don't want to ease up, thank you very much. I pride myself on setting a stimulating pace, and that's what I'm going to do. So if you'll just play the music I've asked for . . . '

She turned her microphone on and addressed the dancers. 'There's a fast dance coming up for anyone who'd like to try it.' She had no need to add that he was interfering again; her thunderous expression already implied it.

'As long as you're sure . . . '

'Of course I'm sure. We women aren't like you men; we don't take to our beds at the first little twinge. Isn't that right, girls?'

A roar of agreement rose up from the floor and Ken had no choice but to respond with a defeated shrug.

'There are times when I'm seriously worried about you,' he returned, keying the music in, 'but go easy on the variations. We don't want the evening marred by any sudden casualties.'

He may as well not have bothered speaking. In fact, he thought ruefully, it would probably have been better if he hadn't. Lisa seemed to take his words as a challenge and deliberately peppered the routine with a succession of high kicks, each one higher and more vigorous than the last. The more athletic members of her class soon followed her lead, and within minutes the dance had escalated into a competition.

Clearly not wishing to be outdone by

her students, Lisa introduced a few extra twirls and the odd jump or two. Then, egged on by a barrage of cheers and whistles, she launched into some serious showing off.

He'd been wrong to think of her as reckless, Ken decided. That was a complete understatement. She was rash, foolhardy, over-confident . . . and at the rate she was going, that ankle would buckle before the dance was even half over.

'Care to join me, Ken?' she called out. 'Or aren't you up to the challenge?'

He moved forward, but there was no way he was going to subject himself to the indignity of joining her, he thought grimly — showy routines were strictly her province.

He'd intended to walk across the stage and off the other side, but at the exact moment he reached her, she suddenly stumbled and dipped back-wards.

'It's all right,' he said, rushing forward to catch her. 'I've got you.'

Her squeal of panic brought the rest of the dancers to a halt.

'Take a deep breath and calm down,' he instructed, his mouth close to her ear. 'And if you want to end the evening with your ankle intact, you'll stop this blatant exhibitionism right now.'

She pushed against him, struggling to stand upright. 'My ankle's fine. So let go of me, please. I want to finish the dance.'

'Not a good idea — ' Ignoring his protests, he swept her up into his arms and carried her bodily off the stage, to the accompaniment of a gale of disbelieving laughter.

'What do you think you're doing?' she yelled, kicking her legs.

'You can stop that right now,' he told her, equally determined, 'or I might be tempted to drop you.'

For some reason that seemed to do the trick and she relaxed against him with her arms around his neck.

On reaching the sound system he sank back on to the stool, with Lisa still in his arms.

'Please, don't go issuing any more challenges like that,' he said, quickly fading the music. 'I'm not sure my heart can stand it.'

She tipped her microphone away from her mouth. 'There was absolutely no need for that. I wasn't hurt, so why couldn't you have left me to finish the dance?'

'And have you fall flat on your back in full view of the Press? That wouldn't do a lot for your image, now would it?'

She gave a small gasp. 'The Press are here?'

'They have been for several minutes. So perhaps it would be a good idea to get off my lap and go down there and speak to them.'

She was on her feet in an instant.

'You've probably noticed that we have two gentlemen from the local paper here with us tonight,' she announced into her microphone, her words immediately restoring order. 'So while I take a few minutes out to give a

189

brief interview, I'll leave you in the very capable hands of our resident caveman, Ken.'

Ken blinked. She expected him to step in and take over the class?

'So, what do I do?' he called after her.

'What do you want to do?' she parried.

'I don't know.'

She turned, and smiled sweetly. 'And I thought you knew everything.'

Serves him right, she thought as she left the stage. And perhaps when he realises that being in charge of a class isn't as easy as it looks, he'll stop interfering and leave me to make the decisions.

The photographer had already taken several shots of the dancers, and only needed a couple of Lisa by herself, and the answers to a few questions.

When she returned to the ballroom, her students were rocking with laughter while Ken regaled them with a stream of jokes. It wasn't quite what she'd had in mind, but she supposed it went some way towards backing up Yvette's claim that the classes were incredible fun.

It was a sentiment held by the majority of the dancers, it seemed, for once the class came to an end, Lisa quickly lost count of the number of people who came up to congratulate her.

'We love the dances, and that DJ of yours is a riot,' one woman told her. 'We're so glad we came along.'

All in all everything had gone rather well, and with Philip's return scheduled for the next day, she'd sleep easy in her bed tonight.

'Can I offer you a lift again, dear?' Yvette asked, as Lisa helped Ken stack the equipment in the cupboard. 'I don't mind waiting while you finish tidying up here.'

'Thank you, Yvette — ' Lisa began, but Ken interrupted.

'No need for that. I'll see Lisa home,' he said. 'There's something we need to talk about.'

'It looks as thought the decision's been take out of my hands,' Lisa said with a rueful smile.

Yvette smiled back, but the glance she gave Ken was unmistakably conspiratorial. Surely Yvette didn't think she was aiding a budding romance? Oh, goodness! This was so embarrassing.

Ken straightened. 'We'll see you again on Tuesday then, shall we?' he said, still looking at Yvette. Then obviously mindful of his promise to be nice to her, he stood up and walked her to the door.

'So what did you want to talk to me about?' Lisa asked when he got back. 'I hope you're not hoping to talk me out of marrying Philip.'

He looked surprised. 'To what end?'

'So you could continue kissing me with a clear conscience?'

He shook his head. 'I'm an unscrupulous businessman, remember? And we both know they don't have consciences.'

'Well, I do, and I'm telling you now,

I'm officially engaged to Philip, whether you like it or not, so you and I won't be sharing any more kisses.'

'Maybe you should try telling that to yourself. From what I recall of the other night, you were the one making the advances.'

'And you're the one arranging all these secluded meetings. I only hope your offer of a lift home isn't just another of your ploys.'

He gave her a pitying smile and shook his head. 'You're leaping to conclusions again. You can rest assured, Lisa, that whatever fantasies you're harbouring, you have absolutely nothing to worry about. I have no intention of trying to talk you out of marrying Philip.'

Embarrassment brought a rush of heat to her face. Talk about misreading the situation!

'You haven't?' She wondered why the discovery didn't please her.

'No. I thought that giving you a lift would give us the opportunity to discuss plan number two, since we didn't get round to it the other night.'

She tossed her Stetson in the cupboard with the rest of her equipment.

'We could have discussed it before yesterday's class, if you'd taken the trouble to turn up.'

He made a helpless little gesture. 'I had an urgent appointment with my builder.'

Yeah, right. She locked the door and withdrew the key.

'And does this builder have long red hair, by any chance?'

A muscle twitched beside his mouth. 'He could do, I suppose. I haven't really taken that much notice. He's usually wearing a cap.'

She stood up. 'And a short blue halter-neck dress?'

His composure never wavered. 'I'm not sure he has the legs for something like that. So, no, probably not.' His eyes were teasing again.

*　★　★

He didn't refer to the matter again until they were in his car and approaching the small row of shops where she'd spotted him the previous day.

'And after the meeting with my builder, I went to visit my cousin.'

'Really?' Her voice was heavy with sarcasm. 'And am I supposed to read any special significance into that?'

Just then, he slowed down and parked opposite the shops.

'Are you going to answer that?' Lisa persisted, her patience beginning to wear thin. 'Or would that spoil the mystery, too?'

He leaned over and opened her door. 'Step outside, and I'll explain.'

Although early July, a cool breeze drifted in from the sea, and Lisa began to wish she'd brought a coat.

'I hope you don't intend keeping me here long,' she said, as he walked round to join her. 'I'm expecting a phone call from Philip and I'd like to be home by midnight.'

'And so you shall be.'

Warm hands encircled her arms and steered her across the forecourt into the shelter of a small grove of trees. Apart from the steady throb of disco music reverberating from a nearby club, there was a complete absence of activity in the area, and Lisa wondered again why he had brought her here. He dropped his hands and stood beside her.

'My cousin Daisy owns these shops and runs the ice-cream parlour. It was her I went to see.'

Lisa found herself smiling again.

'Daisy of the red hair and short blue dress, I take it?'

'Got it in one. It occurred to me, a day or two ago, that the forecourt of Daisy's shops, being large and circular, would be the ideal place for a dance demonstration. I've arranged with Daisy for you to hold one.'

First Yvette and now this. This had to be her lucky day. She felt an overwhelming urge to hug him, but with a supreme effort of will managed to keep her arms clenched firmly at her sides.

'Thank you, Ken,' she said, turning to face him. 'That's wonderful. You've truly redeemed yourself.'

He gave a modest smile. 'And bearing in mind your need to strike while the iron's hot, Daisy's expecting us a week on Sunday.'

She felt her smile slip. 'You're joking! It'll be Tuesday before I get to speak to the class — I can't organise a dance demonstration in only four days.'

'Of course you can,' he said bracingly. 'There's no need for special costumes or routines — or even a polished team. Just put out a general invitation to whoever is willing to turn up and we'll lead the public in a fun dance-along. What could be simpler than that?'

'How do you manage to come up with such perfect ideas?' she asked. 'I thought inviting the newspaper was inspired, but this is pure genius!'

He grinned. 'Years ago, all this was a

dance hall, and one of my mother's favourite haunts. I just thought it could be used for its previous role again — provided people don't mind dancing in the open air.'

As if on cue, the throbbing disco beat subsided and melted into a dreamy ballad. 'May I have the pleasure of this dance?' came Ken's voice, close to her ear. 'An old-fashioned waltz, I believe.'

The sheer unexpectedness of his words caused her to whirl around.

'You want me to dance with you?' She searched his face for amusement and was surprised to find none. 'Here? This very minute?'

He brushed her fingers with his lips. 'A few hours ago you invited me to dance with you,' he murmured. 'I'd like to return the compliment.'

She swallowed. Common sense urged her to pull away from him, to end this game right now. But when he raised his head to meet her gaze, she found herself moving closer.

He slid a hand down her spine,

causing her heart to perform a wild, erratic dance of its own.

With a sigh she moulded her body to his, and together they moved across the moonlit plaza, the spicy scent of his aftershave swirling around them, his soft warmth pervading her skin. She'd danced with plenty of men before, but it had never felt like this. So warm, so exciting and so . . . right. So right, in fact, that when his mouth settled over hers in a devastatingly tender kiss, she made no move to stop him.

Then, before she could respond, he abruptly broke contact.

'I'd better get you home,' he said his voice unusually husky. 'Before you turn into a pumpkin.'

Neither of them spoke much on the way home.

'Have a nice weekend,' Ken said when he pulled up outside her flat. 'Philip will be home, I take it?'

She waited for her heart to leap at the prospect but it didn't.

'Only until Monday, but it will be

nice to have him back. We'll be able to start on our wedding plans.'

She searched his profile for some indication that her words might have affected his peace of mind, but his expression remained impassive.

'You'd better hurry up if you want to catch that phone call,' he said.

'See you Tuesday then,' she answered, feeling oddly reluctant to part with him. Swiftly quashing the feeling, she opened the door and walked away.

She heard her phone ringing as she slipped her key in the lock. Philip would wonder why she wasn't there to answer it. How much of the truth could she safely tell him?

'Been dancing around the flat?' he asked, after they'd exchanged customary greetings. 'You sound out of breath.'

She gave a light laugh. 'Put it down to excitement. My student numbers have almost doubled since Tuesday and Ken's come up with two brilliant ideas for boosting them even higher.'

'I'm pleased one of us has had a good

day.' He gave a long, drawn-out sigh. 'Mine's been a nightmare from start to finish. In fact, it's been a pretty stressful week all round.'

She knew the feeling. 'But it's behind you now and you've got a nice, relaxing weekend with me to look forward to,' she said encouragingly.

'Unfortunately, I haven't. There's something dodgy going on at the company I'm auditing. I suspect a fraud, but won't know until I can spend a day in their office on my own. So I'm doing that tomorrow.'

'You're not coming home?' Disappointment spiralled through her.

'Not this weekend. I've sent the audit team home, but I'll have to stay. It's down to me to get this sorted, and I can't do that with the company's financial director around.'

'So you won't be back until this time next week?'

'That's assuming I get finished by five o'clock. If it's any later I'll probably stay over and travel on the Saturday morning. But I'll be able to see you in the evening as usual, after I've caught up on my sleep.'

She'd been hoping Philip might suggest choosing her engagement ring in the afternoon — but then again, perhaps he'd already bought one in Manchester and intended to surprise her?

If that was the case, she thought, it might be an appropriate point to spring a little surprise of her own, and show him that his mother wasn't the only one who could play the sophisticated hostess.

'Why don't I cook you a special celebratory dinner?' she suggested. 'If you don't come round for a proper meal soon, you'll be thinking that I can't cook.'

And he'd be right, she thought glumly as she hung up the phone. How on earth was she going to put on an impressive three-course meal when she'd never had a cookery lesson in her life?

A Picnic

A phone call to her mother early the next morning provided her with detailed instructions for a simple but impressive meal, along with the advice to be sure to have a trial run first.

Having nothing more pressing to claim her attention, Lisa decided to take the bull by the horns. She'd buy her ingredients at Sandford market that morning and try out her mother's menu during the afternoon.

Despite the demands of the previous evening, Ken's fears had turned out to be unfounded and her ankle was none the worse for her impromptu demonstration. But knowing she shouldn't push her luck too far, she walked the short distance to the market, then lugged her bulging carrier bags over to the bus stop.

She hadn't been there long when

a car pulled up.

'I'm going your way, if you'd like a lift,' Yvette's voice called through the open window. 'You seem to be pretty loaded.'

With a grateful smile, Lisa got in beside her. After exchanging a few pleasantries she explained the reason for her weighty shopping.

'And Philip's not home until this time next week?' Yvette sounded sympathetic. 'That must have put a damper on your weekend. Maybe Ken will call round and take you out somewhere. It'd be a shame to spend all your spare time cooped up in your flat on such a lovely day.'

So innocently phrased, but Lisa could see exactly where Yvette was heading.

'Ken and I are only business colleagues,' she said firmly. 'And to be honest, we don't have all that much in common.'

'Not much in common, you say?' Yvette gave a shrewd smile. 'And here I was thinking you were opposite sides of the same coin. Isn't it funny how wrong you can be?'

Lisa had an early lunch, then, as the weather was far too hot to spend the afternoon in her kitchen, she decided to relax in the garden instead. The students who lived in the upstairs flat had left for the long vacation, so she would be able to sit in the sun and read through her latest batch of dance scripts without fear of being disturbed.

She'd changed into her bikini and was searching her bedroom for a bottle of sun cream when the doorbell chimed.

She'd ignore it, she decided, continuing her search for the sun cream. She wasn't expecting anyone, so whoever it was could go away.

No such luck. The ringing increased in intensity until it was impossible to ignore. With a sigh, she slipped on a pair of flip-flops and walked swiftly down the hall.

She wasn't in. Disappointment gathered in Ken's chest. He'd been a fool to expect she would be. Several hours had elapsed since she'd spoken to his mother, and who was to say what had cropped up in the meantime? His common sense should have told him that someone as outgoing as Lisa was hardly likely to be at home cooking on a day like this. She'd probably gone out with some friends.

He pushed the bell again, and then pressed his face to the glass, willing her to appear. She'd hardly been out of his thoughts since they'd parted last night and he wanted to spend more time in her company.

Nothing.

He tried once more, surprised at the severity of his disappointment. Then, just as he was about to give up and head back to the hotel, a slender figure appeared in the hallway.

'Ken,' she gasped when she opened

the door. 'I wasn't expecting to see you again until Tuesday.'

He didn't answer. He couldn't. The combination of shimmering bikini, rippling hair, and soft, feminine curves had drastically altered the trend of his thoughts.

He resisted the instinct to sweep her into his arms and kiss her into oblivion. Caveman tactics didn't go down well with her — a lesson he'd learned to his cost the previous day.

'I wondered if you'd like to share a picnic with me,' he murmured, letting go of the fantasy. 'I thought your comments the other day might have betrayed a secret yearning.'

A look of interest entered her eyes — only to be replaced by one of regret.

'What about Philip?'

'I'd prefer it to be just the two of us.'

She gave a tiny smile. 'What I meant was, how do you know I'm not about to go out with him? We are engaged, after all.'

That word again. She seemed determined to ram it down his throat at every opportunity. But until things were official and she was actually wearing Philip's ring, Ken wasn't going to take it seriously.

'He's such a conscientious young man, I assumed he'd be working.'

She seemed happy to accept that. 'He is, as it happens. But how will he feel when it gets back to him that I've been picnicking with you?'

A good point, but easy enough to deal with. 'All right, we'll eat it here, where no-one can see us.'

'I don't think that's a good idea either.' A hint of pink stained her cheeks.

'Does that mean you won't be joining me?'

'I'm sorry, Ken, but the answer's no.'

Despite the firmness of her words, she did nothing to bring the conversation to an end. A spark of hope flickered within him.

'It isn't a date,' he said easily. 'I've

come to discuss idea number three, and the nibbles are simply a way of making the meeting more interesting.'

She bit her lip. 'If this idea's anything like the last two, then I suppose I ought to hear it.'

'Most definitely,' he said, his gaze never leaving her face. 'It's an opportunity not to be missed.'

'All right, you've convinced me.' She flung the door wide. 'I'll be ready in two minutes. Come inside while I fling on some clothes.'

He watched her tanned figure walk back down the hall, rather wishing she'd stick with the bikini.

'So where are you taking me?' she asked, once they were seated in his car. 'You do have somewhere in mind, I take it?'

He started the engine and pulled away from the kerb.

'Business plan number three involves a possible new venue for your classes. I thought we'd look the place over first, then swap opinions over the picnic.'

'I'll be surprised if you've managed to come up with somewhere I haven't considered already. I'm well clued up about the places around here and I've been pretty thorough in my investigations.'

'You won't have come across this one. It's part of an old-style nightclub at the southern end of the resort and hasn't come in for much attention in recent years.

'The Sands?'

'That's the one. It has the advantage of two function rooms — '

'And both too small for my needs,' she said wearily. 'I've already seen it, Ken — it's a definite non-starter.'

'Maybe not.' He lowered his voice to a confidential tone. 'But according to my builder, who's just spent several months working on the site, the main function room has been extended and is now of a similar size to the hotel ballroom.'

'That doesn't mean it's open to bookings though — it might need completely refitting.'

'It did, but that's almost finished. They're not showing people round yet, but my builder's had a word with the management and they've granted us a special preview.'

'I see.'

She didn't sound too delighted at the prospect. She probably felt a bit miffed that she hadn't been the one to come up with the information, especially when she'd claimed to be so au fait with the locality.

'And it meets all my requirements?' she asked.

A difficult question. 'Only you can be the judge of that. But from what I've heard, I'd say it does.'

He paused at a red light and took the opportunity to study her expression. The prospect of moving still seemed to hang heavy over her. Maybe she'd miss him more than she was letting on.

The light changed to green. Reluctantly he returned his attention to the road. It was just wishful thinking, he told himself with a rueful smile. She'd made no secret of the fact that she found him interfering and irksome and much preferred the dull predictability of Philip the paragon.

* * *

The reception room had not only been extended, but also redecorated to offer both comfort and style.

'So what do you think?' he ventured, as they followed the manager through the doorway. 'Pretty impressive, wouldn't you say?'

'We're expecting it to be very popular,' the manager told them. 'Would you like us to pencil you in?'

Lisa shook her head. 'I'm sorry, it's a beautiful room, but the carpet covers most of the floor and there's only a tiny area left for dancing.'

Outside, Ken caught her hands in his and gave a deep, regretful sigh.

'What can I say? It had all the qualities you were looking for except the most essential one. I can't believe I overlooked something so basic.'

'Don't worry about it,' she said pleasantly. 'The carpet probably hadn't been fitted when your builder last saw the place. It was an easy enough mistake to make.'

Ken released her hands and shook his head. 'Next time, I'll make a point of asking the right questions before I drag you off for a viewing.'

She didn't argue with that. Did that mean she'd be happy to accompany him to other possible venues? Her smile gave every indication that she would.

'But enough of that,' he said not allowing her to give the matter any more thought. 'Let's forget about business and find a nice, secluded spot for our picnic.'

Uncertainty creased her brow. He'd better rephrase that.

'What I meant to say was — meeting adjourned for light refreshments, and we'll continue our discussion while we eat.'

'That sounds like a good idea,' she replied with an approving smile.

The picnic turned out to be more than a good idea. It was relaxing and cosy, exhilarating and exciting — in fact, it was a heady mixture of indefinable emotions all blended into one.

Reclining on a soft rug spread on a grassy dune overlooking the ocean, they ate a leisurely picnic and talked about anything but business. And the more they talked the more Lisa's eyes sparkled, and the more animated she became. They shared their hopes; their ambitions; traded stories of their childhoods; and after one particularly amusing anecdote concerning Ken's long-gone, but much-missed family cat, he caught her gazing at him from under her lashes, an unidentifiable expression on her face. What was she thinking?

'A penny for them,' he ventured, but she merely gave a wistful smile and began to relate an anecdote of her own.

Suddenly he didn't want to talk. He

wanted to feel those lips against his, to bury his fingers in those soft dark curls . . . to make her want him instead of Philip.

It took every ounce of willpower to resist, but he knew that if he didn't, he'd blow the only chance he'd ever have of becoming her friend. Not that friendship was his only goal, but neither was a fling. He was falling for Lisa in a big way, and if he had any hope of convincing her that he was equally as dependable and reliable as the woefully inadequate Philip, then straightforward friendship was an excellent place to start.

By the time he dropped her back at her flat, they were getting along so well that he was convinced he'd begun to make some headway. She seemed as reluctant as he was to bring the afternoon to a close, and regarded him with such a regretful expression that he was tempted to invite her to have dinner with him.

This is supposed to be a business

meeting, remember? an inner voice cautioned. You've forged the beginnings of a tentative, but fragile friendship today. Push your luck and you risk throwing it away.

'I'd better get back to the hotel,' he said, snatching a glance at his watch. 'We're low on bar staff and I ought to step in. I hope the experience at the Sands hasn't left you feeling too despondent.'

She made to get out of the car. 'Don't worry, Ken. I've been on more than a few wild goose chases over the last few months, and wasted afternoons are par for the course.'

Her words cut straight to his heart. Was that all the afternoon had been to her, an unfortunate waste of time? He looked at her for a long moment, wondering how he could have got things so wrong. To his mind they'd had nothing short of a scintillating afternoon, and he couldn't think of a time when he'd enjoyed himself more. But now, it seemed, the enjoyment had been strictly one-sided and the laughter they'd shared, the confidences they'd exchanged, all counted for nothing in her eyes.

'Don't give up yet,' he said, not sure whether he was speaking to himself or to her. 'Next time, I'll take you somewhere with a generous dance floor, and I'll be sure to enquire about any plans for a carpet.'

Next time? Lisa was about to say she doubted there would be a next time, and then quickly thought better of it. Let him widen his search if he had a mind to. At least then he might finally realise that she'd been right all along and there really was nowhere that could match the Cliff Hotel.

'Yes, you do that,' she said, with her most charming smile. 'I'll look forward to seeing what you come up with.'

* * *

By the end of the week she was on a high. Ken had whisked her off to look at three potential alternatives and each had turned out to have at least one major flaw.

She didn't point out the problems to him immediately, of course. That would have made it seem as though she was dismissing them out of hand. So she'd allowed him to buy her a meal at the restaurant with the unusually spacious function room at the back, before pointing out that the volume of her music would be a little overpowering for the diners.

And she'd been careful not to come down too heavily on the disused warehouse on the outskirts of town. She'd waited until she and Ken were settled in a cosy village pub, before explaining the drawbacks of a concrete floor and complete lack of a bar.

There had been only one worrying moment: the last of the three places they'd looked at, a room above a large supermarket, had seemed as though it might fit the bill. Previously owned by a ballroom dance instructor, it had an oak-sprung floor, generous dimensions, and even a bar. But then Lisa had spotted a large supporting pillar slap-bang in the centre of the dance floor, which, while not posing a problem for its previous occupants, would make line dancing impossible.

She hadn't the heart to point it out to Ken there and then, so had agreed to accompany him to a nearby coffee shop, where she'd broken the news over a plate of cream cakes and two frothy cappuccinos.

She hoped that would be the end of the quest. Although she'd enjoyed the trips and been touched by Ken's efforts, the only thing that could truly make her happy was the news that Ken had changed his mind and was allowing her to stay on at the Cliff Hotel.

She said as much to Philip when he came to dinner on Saturday.

'Is it really necessary to begin every sentence with 'Ken'?' he grumbled. 'I've only been here an hour and all I've had is 'Ken this . . . Ken that'. I'm sick of hearing about him.'

Which was hardly fair, considering Lisa had spent most of that hour listening to details of the fraud at the engineering factory, and Ken's name had only cropped up once or twice.

'Enough of my business plans then,' she said, aiming for a swift change of subject. 'Have you told your parents about our engagement, or are you waiting until I've got my ring?'

'I thought it might be better if they had a chance to get to know you first,' Philip answered a little apologetically. 'I know that technically you've already met my mother, but you hardly had a chance to exchange more than a few words before she had to go.'

'So . . . ?'

'So you're invited to lunch tomorrow.'

'Tomorrow!' She'd be a bit pushed for time. But it was good news, wasn't it? It meant Philip had managed to talk his mother round and that she'd deemed

Lisa worthy of a second chance.

'I've a dance demonstration scheduled for the afternoon, but I can come to lunch first, as long as your parents won't mind me leaving straight afterwards, and you can drop me off at the venue.'

'I can't see that being a problem. I've some work to finish in the afternoon, so that should suit us both. Now, did I tell you that the financial director of this company I was auditing was actually involved in the fraud? There were phoney invoices cropping up from non-existent firms. All done on computer, of course . . . '

By the time he'd finished eating, Philip was showing signs of weariness, and didn't take any persuading to move over to the settee.

'This is nice,' he said, settling down next to her. 'It's a long time since we've had a quiet evening together.'

She sighed and relaxed against him. 'Too long,' she answered, waiting for her heart to respond with a gentle flutter. 'Did you miss me?'

Before he could answer, a loud rap at the door made him frown. 'Are you expecting someone?'

No, she wasn't, but since the rapping was growing increasingly persistent, she had no choice but to go and answer it.

When she threw open the door, there was Ken, bearing a large cardboard box and sporting a sheepish grin.

No, this couldn't be happening . . . Please don't let him be standing there with another of Franco's carry-outs. Not when she'd specifically told him she and Philip had planned a cosy night in.

'You'll have to go,' she told him, wondering what Philip would make of the visit. 'Philip's here and we've just finished eating.'

'Good.' He stepped into the hall. 'That means you're not likely to be going out.'

She attempted to block his way. 'And it also means we're not open to receiving visitors. So would you please go away?'

He raised an eyebrow. 'You might regret saying that when you see what I've brought.'

'I doubt it.'

'You're heartless, you know that?'

Something about his expression made her step back. 'All right. You've got exactly two minutes to convince me, and then I'm throwing you out.'

He gave a brief nod and continued to the living-room.

It took a few seconds for Philip to find his voice.

'Really, Lisa, I didn't expect a visit from him,' he said, with a pained expression. 'Surely whatever he wants can wait?'

'Apparently not.' Lisa made a space on the coffee table and gestured for Ken to put down his box. 'You'd better hurry — you have exactly one minute, thirty seconds left.'

When he lifted the lid, everything inside her went still. She'd been expecting to see pizzas with homemade coleslaw — not two tiny black and white kittens.

Philip jumped to his feet and backed away.

'Scaredy-Cat's disappeared,' Ken said, his voice unusually serious. 'And I was hoping you might agree to become their foster mum.'

Her throat tightened. They were so heart-rendingly small and vulnerable. How could she possibly turn them away?

'Of course I will,' she said. 'Just tell me what you want me to do.'

Philip heaved a sigh. 'Lisa, think about this before you go rushing in with the Good Samaritan act. They might look like a couple of cuddly toys, but they'll wreak havoc on your flat.'

'I don't mind if they do.' She sat down on the settee and lifted a drowsy kitten on to her knee. 'At least that'll mean they're thriving.'

Ken transferred the box on to the settee, and eased himself into the remaining space.

'I think you'll find they're not quite at the havoc-wreaking stage just yet.' He stroked the remaining kitten under the chin. 'They're walking on all four legs, but hopelessly uncoordinated.'

At that, the kitten on Lisa's knee took a few wobbly steps across the settee, and promptly collapsed.

'Oh, just look at them, Philip,' she said, picking it up and placing it back in her lap. 'The poor little things are nowhere near old enough to leave their mum.'

'I'm hoping she might still come back,' Ken told her. 'I've contacted the roads department and there's been no reports of any cats being run over, so I'm trying to stay optimistic. But in the meantime, of course, her kittens need feeding which is where the foster mother bit comes in.'

A surge of panic tightened Lisa's chest.

'If they've been living on their mother's milk, what on earth am I going to feed them? They won't be ready for commercial kitten food.'

Ken lifted a small glass jar out of his jacket pocket.

'According to the vet, the answer is baby food. Let's see if we can tempt them.'

He unscrewed the lid and dipped in a finger. Then, making encouraging noises, he slowly reached into the box and held a blob of food under the kitten's nose.

The kitten lifted its head and issued a plaintive meow.

'This one is the more timid of the two,' Ken said, smearing a splodge of food on the kitten's paw, 'but I'm determined to entice her.'

Lisa held her breath, willing the kitten to show some interest.

Philip slumped into the vacant chair.

'You seem to know a lot about raising orphaned kittens — why don't you take them home with you?'

'I would if I could,' Ken answered, his voice full of regret, 'but my flat has a 'no-pets' clause in its lease, so I can't.'

Lisa shot Philip a glare. 'If this is boring you, why don't you refill the kettle and make us all coffee?'

His mouth dropped open. 'That's rich! *He* barges in on my special homecoming dinner and you're treating *me* like the interloper!'

Lisa couldn't believe he could be so uncharitable.

'You don't like animals much, do you, Philip?' She glanced back at the tiny kittens and sighed. 'Not even the fluffy, helpless kind.'

He gave a dismissive shrug. 'Not really. Considering they're full of lice and fleas, I can never see why they evoke such sympathy.'

She studied his expression for a sign that he might be joking — but none was forthcoming. Swallowing a surge of unease, she returned her attention to the kittens.

'Come on, Fraidy-Cat,' Lisa whispered to the kitten in the box. 'We can't run to a T-bone steak but we've got you some lovely chicken broth.'

The kitten lifted her paw to her face, and poked out a tiny pink tongue.

What a pity Ken wasn't able to have the kittens at home with him, Lisa thought as they exchanged delighted smiles. He was so good with them and obviously cared deeply about their welfare.

Ken handed her the jar. 'Here, you give her brother a splodge while I get their stuff out of the car. If we pour some food in a feeding bowl, we might have them eating properly by the end of the evening.'

At which point the kitten in question left Lisa's knee and set out across the settee again. She caught it just before it tumbled over the edge.

'I can see that one being trouble,' Ken called over his shoulder.

'I can see them both being trouble,' Philip muttered as Ken left the room. 'Listen, Lisa, you don't have to fall for this. There are animal charities that will happily step in — all it would take

228

is a phone call.'

She ignored him and dripped a small quantity of chicken broth on to each of the kitten's front paws. 'Come on, sweetie, eat this for me.'

Philip made an exasperated sound and got to his feet. 'I'll pick you up at twelve tomorrow — if you can manage to prise yourself away.'

'You're going?'

'Well, I'm not hanging round here while you dance attendance on a couple of pampered pets!'

'Pampered? Philip, have a heart. These two have just lost their mother! All I'm doing is trying to compensate.'

Her words were met with silence. Philip had already left.

★ ★ ★

Two minutes later Ken was back, carrying a litter tray, a bag of litter and an assortment of baby and kitten food.

'Philip been taking the happy pills again?'

'I think he felt a bit pushed out. He was expecting my undivided attention and suddenly found himself taking a back seat.'

'I'm sorry if I spoilt your evening.' He poured a little of the food into a shallow bowl. 'Come on, Chaos-Cat,' he said to the adventurer. 'Let's see you get stuck into this.'

For a fleeting moment Lisa wondered if Ken had disrupted her evening on purpose, and had used the kittens as a means of coercing her into spending the evening with him. But one look at his compassionate expression quickly assured her that he was here out of concern for their welfare and had no ulterior motive.

'I don't mind, considering the circumstances, and I'm sure that if Philip hadn't been quite so tired he'd have been a lot more reasonable about it too.'

'Tired or not, I hope he doesn't react like that once you have children. That is, if he actually wants any.'

Lisa tried to picture Philip cooing over a baby, and found it virtually impossible. But that didn't mean he'd be a reluctant father. Three or four years into the future, when his career was established and he was earning a comfortable salary, he'd probably mellow into a devoted family man.

'I'm sure he does, but at his age there are more pressing concerns.'

'And what about you, Lisa?' Ken asked, his eyes intent on her face. 'Do you see yourself having children?'

She tried to picture her future offspring. They could easily inherit her dark curls, and Philip's grey eyes and serious manner. So why did her imagination persist in serving up an image of two lively tots sporting Ken's vivid blue eyes and mischievous expression?

She quickly quashed the image.

'Yes, I'd like children,' she told him. 'Two or three.'

He looked thoughtful. 'I never saw you as the family type,' he said softly. 'I imagined you'd be like my mother, perhaps having just one and then returning to your career as soon as the child could safely be left.'

'I'd never leave anyone else to bring up my children, and if it meant scaling down my career to be with them, then that's what I'd do.'

The discussion was brought to a halt by Chaos-Cat stepping into the food bowl.

'I'd better be going,' Ken said, once they'd cleaned the kitten up and rid the settee of splodges of baby food. 'You've got everything you need to keep these two happy tonight, and I'll bring a proper sleeping basket next time I call round.'

Suddenly the rest of the evening stretched emptily before her and she found herself wanting him to stay.

'I never did get you that coffee. Would you like one now?'

'I can't, I'm afraid.'

'Oh.' For some reason she'd assumed he'd been planning to spend the rest of the evening with her. 'Work, or a prior engagement?'

He got to his feet. 'The Hot Pudding Queen. I'd arranged to be at her house at six o'clock, but Scaredy-Cat's disappearance put paid to that. Still, better late than never.'

She nodded, feeling strangely bereft. 'I'll see you tomorrow at the demonstration, then,' she said. 'Could you bring my Stetson along with everything else from the hotel cupboard? I'm going to Philip's parents' for lunch, so I'll be taking my dance gear with me and changing when I get to the venue.'

He nodded. 'Will do.'

He leant towards her. Heart hammering, she lowered her gaze and waited for the gentle pressure of his lips on hers.

Instead he reached forward to give the kittens one last stroke. 'Be good,' he whispered. They responded with a low, contented purr.

Fraidy-Cat was still purring several minutes after he'd gone.

'So he's managed to charm you too, has he?' Lisa whispered. 'Well, listen to me, young lady. The man is an accomplished flirt and not worthy of such devotion. So you'd do well to abandon that wistful expression, and push him right out of your thoughts.'

Philip's Plans For Lisa

Philip phoned the next morning to check that she would be ready on time.

'And wear something elegant,' he told her. 'Nothing too short.'

'I haven't got anything elegant,' she all but shrieked. 'And with only an hour before you pick me up, there's no time to go out and buy something.' She didn't have the money anyway, but she wasn't about to admit to that.

'In which case, go for subtle and understated. My parents tend to treat Sunday lunches as fairly formal affairs. I don't imagine that you turning up wearing a hair-band for a skirt would go down too well.'

Lisa thought of Ken's appreciative expression when she'd opened the door dressed only in a bikini and smiled at the contrast in attitude. Had Philip always been so narrow-minded or was it only now that she'd begun to notice?

'I'd worked that one out for myself, thank you very much,' she said sharply. 'I'd already decided not to turn up in my dance clothes.'

He sighed. 'I'm sorry,' he said. 'I just want my parents to realise that under all the modern trappings you're an old-fashioned girl at heart.'

'Relax, Philip,' she said wearily. 'If soft and feminine is what your parents want, then that's what they'll get.'

She bid him goodbye and replaced the receiver. The shift dress was washed and ready to wear, but mindful of the Elegant Chignon's aversion to bright and colourful, she decided it might not be appropriate.

However, apart from the sarong that had come with her bikini, or an appliquéd denim gypsy skirt, she had nothing that could safely be described as feminine.

The gypsy skirt it was, then. Perhaps the addition of a crisp white broderie-anglaise blouse would offset the casualness of the denim.

By the time Philip arrived, Lisa was sure she'd made the right decision, and he evidently thought so too, for he greeted her with an affectionate kiss, and even asked after the kittens. This was going to be a very successful day, Lisa told herself as she stepped out into the warm July air, for business as well as pleasure.

Philip's home was an impressive 1930s detached house, tucked away in the older, more exclusive part of Radcliff, and Lisa couldn't help feeling over-awed as the car swept up the drive. If this was the type of house he had in mind for when they were married, no wonder he had to work all the hours God sent. The garden alone would have taken all Lisa earned in a month just to keep it tidy.

She half expected a butler to appear at the door, but it was the Elegant Chignon herself who came to greet them. She swept her gaze over Lisa's clothes, then ran a slender hand down her own slim-fitting, immaculately tailored silk dress.

'What a quaint outfit,' she mused, stepping back to study it in more depth. 'Is it your costume for the dance demonstration?'

'No, it's not,' Philip put in, clearly embarrassed. 'She's going to change into that later, after I've dropped her off.'

His mother offered an apologetic little smile. 'It's difficult to tell with you modern youngsters. You have such novel ways of expressing yourselves. But come through and meet my husband. Can I offer you a drink before we eat?'

'That would be lovely,' Lisa said, determined not to allow the snide remarks to affect her composure. 'I'll have a glass of wine.'

'I think we can arrange that,' said Philip's father, stepping forward to greet her. 'I've got a nice fresh Muscadet that I think you might like.'

At least he was friendly, Lisa thought, sending him a grateful smile.

Lunch was a strained affair. The Elegant Chignon, eager to discuss her passion for antique furniture, insisted on giving a run-down of her recent acquisitions. Lisa felt nothing but relief when Philip's father, adroitly turning the conversation to business, cut the lecture short.

'Lisa, I understand you run a business of sorts,' the Elegant Chignon put in towards the end of the meal.

'That's right,' Lisa said, pleased to be invited to contribute to the conversation at long last. 'It's early days yet, but the signs are it's going to become very successful.'

The Elegant Chignon didn't look too impressed. 'So this is a long-term venture? Not just a stop-gap until you find something better?'

Lisa put down her spoon and dabbed at her mouth with a napkin.

'There *is* nothing better. This is my ideal job and I can't imagine anything else I'd rather do.'

A strained silence hung in the room.

'The thing is . . . ' the Elegant Chignon began, as if addressing a small child. 'It doesn't have a great deal of social standing.'

'Maybe not in the circles you mix in.' Lisa fought down an image of Philip's mother and her cronies attempting to wiggle their hips to a hot Latin rhythm. 'But my friends and family think it's a great career, as do the dozens of students who flock to my classes each week.'

The Elegant Chignon exchanged glances with her husband.

'But once you marry my son, our circle will become your circle, and your occupation will be regarded with some consternation.'

Lisa took a deep breath. 'With respect, I doubt if you really understand what my job involves.'

By way of reply, the Elegant Chignon rose from her chair and crossed the room to a hideous antique sideboard. She pulled open a drawer, then returned to the table brandishing a newspaper cutting, which she placed carefully on Lisa's side plate.

'This is you, I believe,' she said with a superior little smile. 'Now, can you honestly look at that picture and tell me you have a tasteful and dignified career?'

Lisa picked up the cutting with a feeling of dread. What she saw caused her to catch her breath. It was a page from the previous evening's local paper and showed Ken carrying her off the stage of the Cliff hotel — her skirt riding high on her thighs and her head thrown back in a scream. Ken's face, luckily for him, was obscured by his hat. The heading proclaimed: 'Me And My Job — Lisa Gates, Line Dance Instructor.'

Heat flooded her cheeks.

'This picture is as much of a surprise to me as it is to you,' she said, looking to Philip for support. 'That's in no way typical of what goes on at my classes.'

He squeezed her hand. 'Don't worry, Lisa. My parents have come up with a way for you to put this way of life behind you and take up a more fitting occupation.'

She caught her breath. 'Fitting for what?'

He removed his hand and leaned back in his chair. 'For the wife of a well-respected accountant, soon to be promoted to junior partner.'

She swallowed hard. 'Go on,' she urged. 'This I can't wait to hear.'

The Elegant Chignon gave a tight little smile. 'My husband's firm has a vacancy for a full-time receptionist and we'd like to offer the position to you. It would enable you to mix with a better class of person and provide you with a respectable way to fill your time.'

For several seconds, Lisa simply stared.

'Supposing I don't want to give up my dancing to become a receptionist?'

Philip patted her hand. 'Oh, come on, Lisa, you can't be serious. When we met, you were studying business and these classes were just a sideline. It's time to consign them to your student days, where they belong, and concentrate your energies on more deserving matters.'

'Such as your climb to success, I suppose? Listen to me, Philip, and listen hard. I studied business for one reason only . . . to enable me to work as my own boss and run the best dance school I possibly could. The last thing I want is to be shut away in some dreary office doing a job that's too dull-as-ditch-water for words. So I'm sorry, Philip, but I intend to decline your parents' kind offer and continue organising my life as I see fit.'

The Elegant Chignon clutched the edge of the table as if she feared she might pass out.

'I expect you two have a lot to discuss,' she said in a tight voice. 'Your father and I will be in the sitting-room if you need us.'

'Mother, I'm so sorry,' Philip called out as she swept out of the room, her husband trailing obediently in her wake. 'I had no idea Lisa was going to react like this. I'm sure she'll change her mind . . .'

'Not a chance,' Lisa snapped, scrunching the newspaper cutting into a ball. 'And now, if you don't mind, I'd like to go.'

She grabbed her bag and marched out of the door without waiting to see if he followed her. He did, but the hard slam of the door as he climbed into the car told her all she needed to know about his mood.

★ ★ ★

Philip drove in tight-lipped silence until they reached the arcade of shops.

'Here we are,' he said, his voice stilted and remote. 'I'll get your holdall out of the boot.'

She followed him and waited on the pavement. What had made her imagine she could ever be happy with someone like him? He wanted a wife who'd sit placidly by while his needs took precedence. Whereas she wanted a partner who'd value her dreams and ambitions, and give her the freedom to make her own choices.

'I hope it's not too long before you come to your senses.'

'I already have,' she said quietly, 'and things are much clearer now.'

He gave a satisfied smile. 'I thought as much — '

'So I won't be marrying you, Philip, or even seeing you again.'

He slammed down the boot lid. 'You don't mean that . . . '

'Oh, but I do,' she said, her mind brutally clear. 'Meeting your parents today brought home to me how very different you and I are and made me realise that we don't have a future together.'

'If you could only be a little more flexible, Lisa . . . '

'I could turn into the person you want? Well, this might surprise you, Philip, but I like myself just the way I am — and right now it's you I don't much like.'

'I'll pretend I didn't hear that. You're obviously overwrought. We'll talk again when you've had a chance to calm down.'

'There's nothing to talk about.' She gripped her holdall. 'I don't love you and the relationship is over. How difficult is that to understand?'

His face tightened. 'Lisa . . . '

'I wish you well, Philip, and I hope you find the person you're looking for, but it certainly isn't me.'

Without sparing her another glance, he climbed into his car and accelerated away.

She watched his tail lights disappear into the traffic, and then slowly turned to face the arcade of shops. She had a dance demonstration to get through and intended to put all thoughts of Philip exactly where they belonged — firmly at the back of her mind.

★　★　★

A large section of the forecourt had been roped off, but apart from a solitary table and chair under the shade of the trees, there was no indication that a dance demonstration was about to take place. Where was her flag, her sound system and case of CDs, and, most important of all, what had happened to Ken?

'Oh, please don't let me down,' she whispered. 'I'm relying on you to see me through this and I really can't do it without you.'

Fighting back tears, Lisa threaded her way through the loitering holiday-makers and walked wearily into the ice-cream parlour.

'Can I help you?' a chirpy redhead asked. 'You seem a bit lost.'

This had to be Ken's cousin, Daisy. And from her ready smile and sympathetic manner, she was every bit as charming as he was.

Lisa held out her hand. 'Hello, Daisy,' she said, her voice remarkably steady. 'I'm Lisa, the line-dance instructor. I was wondering if Ken had arrived yet.'

Daisy took her hand and shook it warmly. 'Nice to meet you. Ken's not due for another fifteen minutes or so, but come and sit down and I'll get you a drink.'

Lisa gave a sigh of relief. Goodness, what was the matter with her? She hadn't even thought to check the time — she'd just panicked. Daisy must think her a total idiot.

'I ought really to get changed,' she said, attempting to gloss over her mistake. 'I hope you don't mind, but I had an engagement before this and I've brought my dance clothes with me. Is there anywhere I can change?'

'Sure, you can use our staff cloak-room. There's a good-sized mirror and plenty of hot water. I'll take you there now if you like.'

Lisa smiled gratefully. 'Are you going to be joining in the dancing?' she asked as she followed Daisy to the back of the shop. 'No previous experience necessary.'

'I'm what you might describe as rhythmically challenged,' Daisy said, her eyes warm with humour, 'so I'll stick to supplying the refreshments. Let me know when you need to cool off and I'll bring some over to you.' She pushed open a door as she spoke.

'That's very kind.' Lisa followed her into the room and dropped her holdall on to a chair.

'Ken's idea — he's asked me to keep you well supplied with cold drinks and ordered two ice-cream sundaes for the end of the afternoon.'

How very like him, Lisa thought. He had an incredible talent for second-guessing her needs before she even knew what they were. A rare and endearing quality. In fact, she'd discovered an abundance of endearing qualities in him of late. Not only had he proved to be tender, considerate and caring, but also lovable, sexy and funny.

Oh, listen to her . . . anyone would think she was in love with him. Whatever had happened to stubborn and interfering? Wasn't he that too? But if he was, it no longer seemed to matter. He was the one person guaranteed to brighten her day and right now she was desperate to see him.

'I'll look forward to that,' Lisa said, suddenly aware that Daisy was waiting for an answer. 'Ice-cream is my favourite feel-good food.'

Daisy looked pleased. 'I'd better get back to the grindstone. See you soon.' Daisy gave her another bright smile and was gone.

Lisa slumped on to a chair in despair. Falling in love with Ken was the most stupid thing she could have done. He had no interest in her except for a short-term affair and was a classic commitment-phobe.

Maybe Philip was right and she was overwrought. Once she'd had a few minutes on her own to calm down and think things through, she'd see this ridiculous notion for what it was.

Lisa heard the music the minute she stepped back into the shop.

'I'll take care of your holdall,' Daisy offered. 'It's a bit cumbersome to lug around.'

'Thanks,' said Lisa. 'My clothes only took up a small part — the rest's taken up with flyers. I'm hoping to find volunteers to hand them round.'

'You shouldn't have too much trouble — there's quite a crowd.'

Lisa's spirits soared. 'I'd better get a move on then,' she said.

She spotted Ken immediately — his sizzling orange shirt made sure of that.

'Ah, there you are, Lisa,' he announced over the microphone, 'and looking as delectable as ever. Ladies and Gentleman, I give you Lisa Gates — our gorgeous line-dance instructor.'

Tears welled in her eyes. The warmth in his voice was more than mere flattery. It was heartfelt and genuine, and he was clearly as pleased to see her as she was to see him. In that moment, she knew that her first thought had been correct — she really did love him.

In her eagerness to reach him, she

didn't notice the protruding pushchair wheel, and next second, she found herself hurtling towards the ground. This time Ken wasn't near enough to catch her and she hit the pavement with a sickening crack.

★ ★ ★

'Don't try to move . . . ' Lisa opened her eyes to a sea of anxious faces, the most prominent of which was Ken's.

'I'm all right,' she mumbled. 'I just need a few minutes to get my breath back.'

His face creased with concern. 'No, Lisa, I don't think so.'

She shook her head and attempted to sit up. 'If you could help me to my feet . . . I'm sure I'll be all right in a minute.'

'Try sitting up, just for now,' he cautioned, kneeling down to support her. 'Roll on to your side and take the weight on your elbow.'

A searing pain shot through her leg,

causing her to let out a loud gasp.

'I've probably just twisted a muscle,' she panted, reaching down to clutch the offending limb. 'It'll be all right when it's loosened up.'

Ken didn't look convinced. 'From the amount of pain you're in, I'd say you've done more than that. I'm calling an ambulance.'

'No, Ken, please.' Lisa placed her hands on the ground, preparing to lever herself up. 'I'll be fine once I'm on my feet. Just let me . . . '

But this time the pain was so intense she thought she would pass out. She squeezed her eyes tightly shut and gripped Ken's arm, her breath coming fast and ragged.

A murmur of sympathy rippled through the bystanders.

'I'm sorry, Lisa,' Ken said softly, 'but persistence alone won't get you out of this. You need urgent medical attention.'

She gazed up into his eyes, willing him to take her side.

'But if I'm not here the demonstration can't go ahead. Oh, Ken, please don't force me to cancel it.'

Ken took out his mobile phone. 'I'm calling an ambulance.'

The music was still playing when the paramedics lifted Lisa into the ambulance, and despite her pain she couldn't help noticing that her students had done her proud. Resplendent in eye-catching western gear they had turned up in their droves and were attracting a host of favourable comments.

'Ken, keep the demonstration going for me,' she pleaded. 'You've a strong nucleus of experienced dancers there. All you need do is play the music and they'll lead the rest of the group.

'Ken, please,' she urged when he didn't answer. 'This demonstration means a lot to me — I've too much riding on it to cancel it now.'

'I'll sort something out,' he promised as the ambulance doors slammed shut, but his expression was far from convincing.

Twenty minutes later Lisa realised why.

She'd been admitted to accident and emergency and was waiting to be wheeled down to X-ray, when Ken turned up in the treatment bay.

'They wouldn't let me travel in the ambulance with you, so I had to follow in my car.'

Her emotions flickered between pleasure and disappointment. She was indescribably pleased to have him with her, but his presence meant he'd cancelled the demo — and with it, all hope of attracting more students.

'The demo could have gone ahead without me,' she said, blinking back tears. 'All you had to do was work through the play list. No-one would have expected you to dance.'

A hurt look crossed Ken's face. 'You think I'm here because I don't want to dance?' He heaved a sigh. 'Lisa, I've said this before and I'll say it again — when are you going to learn to trust me? I did what any self-respecting manager would do and delegated the task to someone else.'

That wasn't exactly a comforting thought.

'But I wanted you to do it!' she protested. 'That sound system cost me a small fortune. You can't just let anyone operate it. It has to be someone who knows what they're doing.'

'I don't think your friend Yvette would take kindly to being described as 'just anyone',' he said with a hint of amusement. 'According to her, she's stepped in as your DJ before and is more than capable of coping in my absence.'

Yvette! Of course! And who could be better?

'I swear that woman is my fairy godmother — I don't know what I'd do without her.'

'Daisy handed out your flyers. She didn't think you'd mind that she went into your holdall — she knew you wanted them distributed. And before you start worrying, the holdall's in my car, and Daisy has promised to drop your sound system off at the hotel on her way home tonight.'

Gratitude brought a fresh surge of tears to Lisa's eyes.

'Thank you,' she whispered. 'Today's been like a million bad dreams all at once. I don't know how I'd have got through it without you.'

He brushed a strand of hair from her eyes. 'So the lunch didn't go too well, then?'

She couldn't look at him. 'You were right. I was wrong. When it came to the crunch, Philip wasn't anywhere near as loyal as I'd imagined. In fact, he completely failed to take my side. Would you believe he had a plan to turn me into a clone of his mother? The two of them had joined forces to map out my life for me.'

'But you put them straight?' His hand lingered on her shoulder. The warmth from his fingers was making it difficult to concentrate.

'I finished with him,' she said,

resisting the urge to rest her cheek on his hand and sob. 'Oh, Ken, this has been such an awful day!'

He drew her head on to his shoulder and pressed his lips to her forehead.

'Don't worry, I'm here,' he murmured, 'and I'm not planning on going anywhere for a long while yet.'

After the X-ray, Lisa found herself back in the treatment bay.

'Your leg is broken,' the doctor told them. 'You have a closed simple fracture of the femur, and considering the femur is the toughest bone in the body, you must have had some fall.'

She nodded, feeling wretched. This surely spelled the end of her career. There was no way she could teach with her leg in a cast.

'How long will I be out of action?' she whispered, desperate for his answer, yet dreading it at the same time.

'There won't be any need for traction, just immobilisation of the injury until it heals, so you'll be in a cast for about six weeks.'

Six weeks! And she was due out of the hotel in three! There was no hope now of ever being able to make her business so lucrative that Ken would be begging her to stay. It would be a wonder if her business survived at all.

'And then she'll be able to start dancing again?' Ken asked.

'Not immediately,' the doctor said, peering over the top of his spectacles. 'I'd advise gentle walking for the first two weeks after the cast comes off. I wouldn't recommend attempting anything more vigorous for a week or two after that.'

'What am I going to do?' Lisa whispered the moment the doctor had gone. 'I can't take my classes in a full leg cast and without me, they won't be able to continue.'

Ken sat down on a chair by her bed, his gaze lingering on her tear stained-face. She didn't deserve this, he thought. She'd been working so hard to keep her classes afloat and he couldn't imagine a worse blow.

'Hey, what sort of talk is that?' he said gently, tilting her chin with his index finger. 'Just follow my example and delegate.'

Her face had gone deathly pale and her eyes were heavy with despair.

'I've plenty of keen students, but there's no-one I'd trust to take over the classes. It takes weeks of training to get it right.'

'Not even Yvette?'

She glanced up at him, her green eyes dull and despondent.

'Yvette's the exception, I admit, but she only knows a few basic routines. A new dance each week is the minimum my students will expect, and if it's not forthcoming they'll feel disappointed and go elsewhere. Oh, Ken, this is impossible. Even if I manage to find someone to take over, I'm no closer to finding a permanent venue, and you'll need me to be out before I can resume the search.'

He couldn't bear to see her so unhappy.

'This isn't like you,' he said, covering her hand with his. 'What's happened to all the cheery optimism and steely determination?'

Her hands trembled under his. 'I want to carry on, of course I do, but right now I can't see any way round these problems.'

'Supposing I was to say that I wouldn't ask you to leave the hotel until you'd been offered a suitable alternative?'

Her gaze locked with his. 'But how could you possibly agree to that? Your refurbishments have been booked for weeks.'

'I'm an optimist too, Lisa, and if I didn't think you'd be able to find somewhere reasonably close to the deadline, I wouldn't be offering.'

'You really mean it?' she asked, a glow beginning to light her eyes. 'You won't ask me to leave until I find somewhere else?'

'That's right.' The way her face lit up was enough to waylay any doubts. 'But no holding out for an impossible ideal — anything that's half-way decent and I expect you to snap it up.'

She stared at him, tears glistening on her lashes. 'Oh Ken, thank you so much. You've no idea what that means to me.'

He squeezed her hands. 'Oh, I think I do. So stop treating me like the enemy. I'm with you on this, all right?'

She nodded and swallowed hard. 'The minute I get home I'll phone the dance organisation and ask them to find me a relief instructor . . . and maybe another DJ?'

'So you don't think I'm up to scratch?' he demanded, but with a grin.

'I can't expect you to carry on as DJ when I'm not even going to be there,' she offered in a small voice. 'That would be assuming too much.'

'Let me be the judge of that,' he whispered. 'You concentrate on finding a replacement instructor for now. I'm happy to continue as DJ.'

Now what had made him say that, he

wondered as she was wheeled off to the plaster room. Not the part about staying on as DJ — that was something he enjoyed and continuing wouldn't pose any problem. But to say she could extend her stay beyond the eviction date had been totally rash — and well nigh impossible!

The Truth About Yvette

Ken stayed with Lisa while the cast was applied and then took her home in his car. Away from the bustle of the hospital, she felt a strange uneasiness in his company and didn't know whether to be delighted or dismayed when he said he would make her a sandwich and mix the kittens' feed. On the one hand, she longed for time alone to sort out her emotions, and on the other, she desperately wanted him to stay.

But in the end her stomach won out. The Elegant Chignon's meagre portions had hardly been sufficient to see her through the next hour, let alone fuel a stress-ridden afternoon.

So when Ken returned from her kitchen bearing a mountain of the most professional-looking sandwiches she'd ever seen, she took the plate with a smile and relaxed on the settee while he re-acquainted himself with the kittens.

His gentle, sensitive side was very much in evidence tonight and so at odds with Lisa's initial perception of him as an unscrupulous and uncaring businessman, that she began to wonder if she'd read him all wrong. And if she'd been wrong about that, then she could have been wrong about his feelings for her.

'Time I wasn't here,' he said at last. 'Is there anything else I can get you before I go?'

She shook her head, struggling to hide her disappointment. 'I'm sorry if I've held you up,' she said, 'Is there somewhere you have to be?'

'I promised to visit the Hot Pudding Queen.' He carried the kittens' empty food bowl to the kitchen. 'But she's used to me being held up now and then because of work — you know, meetings and such like.'

The woman must be very sure of him, Lisa thought sadly.

'Thank you for staying,' she said,

searching his face for any sign that he might be tempted to stay longer. 'It was really nice of you.'

He grinned. 'No trouble. I couldn't leave the poor kittens to fend for themselves, could I? I'll pop in each day if that's all right. They'll be a bit much for you to cope with as things are at the moment, and you'll have enough on your plate just looking after yourself.'

Of course, the kittens. Lisa's heart sagged. He wasn't here because of any unresolved feelings for her. He was feeling guilty at off-loading the kittens and felt obliged to share the task of looking after them.

'See you tomorrow then.' His fingers brushed her cheek in a gentle caress that sent the blood coursing through her veins. 'And don't rush to the door when you hear the bell. I don't want you having another fall.'

''Bye then,' Lisa answered, forcing herself to look anywhere but at him. 'I hope you enjoy what's left of your evening.' And as the door closed silently behind him it was all she could do not to cry.

★　★　★

By the time Ken arrived the next morning, Lisa had her feelings firmly under control and managed to greet him with a carefree smile.

'I've been in touch with the dance organisation,' she told him, 'and they've promised to send an instructor to tomorrow's class. We've negotiated a fee and provided my student numbers continue to rise, I should have just about enough money to cover my bills.'

He brushed a hand over her hair, sending tiny shivers skipping up and down her spine. 'See? I told you there was no need for doom and gloom. Is this instructor anyone you know?'

'Her name's Simone,' Lisa croaked, her throat suddenly dry, 'and she's only recently joined the organisation.' She paused to take a deep, calming breath. 'But she's attended all the necessary workshops and is pretty well versed in the dances I was planning to teach.'

His palm dropped to her shoulder. 'So all you have to do is concentrate on getting better, and try not to get too bored.'

The warmth from his fingers was searing into her flesh. 'That's going to be the hard part,' she told him, casting around for something suitably mundane to say. 'I'm not used to sitting about — it'll drive me up the wall.'

Whatever had possessed her to say that? It sounded as though she was hinting for him to take her out when nothing could be further from the truth. Coercing him into spending more time with her would simply be storing up trouble. For what future could there be in encouraging the attentions of a man who not only had a significant other in his life already, but also made it his business to flirt with practically every female he met?

★   ★   ★

Whatever Lisa's subconscious intentions, her words must have had some impact for a couple of mornings later, Ken invited her to go for a drive.

'I don't think so,' she said in a voice intended to be brisk, but which came out sad and regretful.

'It's only a drive,' he persisted, stooping to look into her eyes. 'I'm not trying to fix you up with another venue for your classes.'

It might be easier for her to accept if he were, she told herself as she struggled to still her racing heart. Since he had stopped pressurising her to move out of the hotel, she'd missed their little excursions. But if she agreed to an outing that was based on pleasure rather than business, what message would that send out to him? That she didn't mind being added to his list of casual girlfriends?

'Lisa? It would do you good to escape the kittens for a while.'

'I wouldn't mind sitting in on some of my classes,' she admitted.

He glanced down at her cast and gave a rueful smile. 'Maybe when you've had a little more practice at getting around. But just for the moment I'd steer well away from crowds.'

He was right, she thought, and as it was only a drive he was offering, why not go along with him? Surely they should be able to share an outing now and then, and enjoy each other's company?

'Yes, why not?' she agreed. 'Where did you have in mind?'

His smile melted her insides. 'You've a choice between a leisurely drive on the country or the kite festival on the beach.'

She smiled back. 'I'll go for whichever is the shorter journey. This cast gets fairly uncomfortable when I can't shift around in my seat.'

As they sped past the hotel, Lisa couldn't help noticing that there seemed to be a great deal of activity in the vicinity of the old theatre.

'Phase one of my modernisation plans,' Ken told her. 'Now that the kittens have been moved to safe quarters, there's no reason why I can't make a start on the car park.'

He'd been holding off his plans for the sake of the kittens? The more she learned about Ken Huntley, the more she liked him. All that talk about business coming before sentiment had been nothing but a lot of hot air. Ken had inherited his father's tender heart after all.

'The change of scenery must be doing you good,' Ken remarked. 'I haven't seen you smile like that since before your accident.'

'Talking of which,' Lisa answered, retaining an air of private amusement, 'I haven't had a chance to thank Daisy for her help. Would you mind if we stopped off to see her?'

Ken hesitated. He'd been hoping he and Lisa might find somewhere quiet and unhurried where they could have a long, uninterrupted chat. There were things he wanted to say to her, things she needed to know.

But perhaps now wasn't a good time, so soon after Philip.

'I daresay we can just as easily watch the kites from there,' he said, trying not to sound as though he minded.

He parked the car as near to the ice-cream parlour as possible, and then brought her crutches to the passenger door. She hadn't had time to get used to them yet, so her progress was still slow and laborious.

On impulse, he tossed her crutches back into the car and swept her up into his arms. For a moment she looked as if she might protest, but she obviously thought better of it.

'If you drop me, Ken Huntley, I'll — '

It was his cue to make some jocular remark, to counter her threats with some of his own, and draw attention away from the intimacy of the situation. He did none of those things, however. As her eyes locked with his, he slowly lowered his mouth to cover hers and silenced her with a lingering kiss.

When he raised his head, two bright spots had appeared on her cheeks, and her eyes were dreamy and wistful. Maybe today might be a good time to have that chat after all!

There was only one vacant table on the forecourt, and scarcely had Ken commandeered it and settled Lisa, than Daisy came breezing past.

'Hello,' she called out, clearly delighted to see them. 'Ken, there are some stools in the shop — you can bring one for Lisa to rest her leg on.'

'Thanks, Daisy.' Ken passed a menu to Lisa. 'I'll be right back.'

When he returned, Lisa was flipping through the menu with Daisy standing at her elbow, giving a detailed rundown of each of their lines.

'I told Lisa you should have your ice-cream sundaes now,' she said. 'They're already paid for.'

'But they all look so tempting,' Lisa said. 'I can't decide.'

The two of them seemed to be getting on well, Ken thought as he sat beside Lisa. As long as Daisy didn't recount any embarrassing incidents from his childhood, then he supposed he didn't mind. It was good to see Lisa looking more relaxed.

'I'll have a rum and raisin,' he said.

Lisa continued to turn the pages and when she reached the last one, her face lit up.

'Oh, what a lovely idea! Look, Ken, Daisy's put one of my flyers into the back of the menu. Daisy, you're a star.'

Ken gave his cousin an appreciative smile.

'Actually, it's Ken's mother you ought to be thanking,' Daisy confided. 'It was her idea. She spent ages adding them to the menus and even stuck a few up by the till.'

'Really?' Lisa shot Ken a questioning look. 'I had no idea Ken's mother was so concerned about promoting my business.'

'Concerned?' Daisy laughed. 'If you

ask me, the woman's obsessed. But then, Aunt Yvette was never one to do things by halves — it's always been all or nothing with her, hasn't it, Ken?'

Ken didn't respond. He couldn't. This was one of those rare occasions in his life when he was completely stuck for words.

'Ken?'

He glanced up and looked away again at once.

Daisy gave him an affectionate nudge. 'Hey, I wasn't criticising her! It's just that Aunt Yvette's the type to throw herself heart and soul into everything, and loves to have a cause to champion.'

Ken didn't like the way Lisa was looking at him — it was a combination of accusation, distrust and disappointment.

'I know what you meant,' he said. 'How about you scoot off and bring us both a rum and raisin, Daisy? Otherwise we'll be here all day.'

★ ★ ★

'I thought your mother was dead,' Lisa hissed when Daisy had left. 'Why didn't you tell me that she's Yvette?'

He sighed. 'I suppose I was trying to pre-empt a situation that could have spiralled out of control. My mother didn't die, Lisa, and I never intended you to think that she had.'

'But you implied that she was ill, that her health had taken a turn for the worse ... but from the amount of energy she puts into her dancing I don't see much evidence of that.'

Scepticism laced her words, and he knew that he'd have trouble convincing her he was telling the truth, but he owed it to her to try.

'When my mother closed down her dance school,' he said slowly, 'it was partly because of dwindling numbers and partly because she could no longer see well enough to teach. She had advanced cataracts and needed an operation, but she was so worried about something going wrong that she wouldn't agree to it.

'Then, a few years later, when my father was told he needed a heart by-pass, she realised she would need all her faculties to look after him, so she plucked up her courage and had the operation done.'

Lisa looked a little shame-faced. 'That was very brave of her — and so unselfish, too. Your mother's a remarkable woman.'

He gave a brisk nod. 'The upshot of it was, her operation was successful, but my father wasn't so lucky and he suffered several more years of poor health before he died.'

'And she spent her time looking after him?'

'Not entirely. There were days when he was able to get into the hotel and continue working as manager. But she was his rock, and once he'd gone, she felt completely redundant. Your classes, coming when they did, opened up a whole new interest, and the fact that they were held at her old stomping ground no doubt doubled the attraction.'

'So what are you saying?' she asked when he fell silent.

'When I saw her at your classes I was worried that if you realised who she was, you might let her persuade you that you had a fighting chance of staying on at the hotel.'

'And would that have been so very terrible?'

'It would have raised your hopes only to have them dashed. Like my father, my mother tends to place sentiment before business, whatever the long-term cost. An alliance with her would have ended in tears, which was why I made her promise not to mention the family connection and urged her to keep a low profile.

'She loves your classes, Lisa,' he said, searching her face for evidence that she understood, 'and I've hated having to tell her over and over that they can't continue at the hotel.'

'In which case,' she said gently, 'I hope you've since told her that my leaving has become a little more flexible?'

'Not yet,' he murmured, desperate to evade the topic.

She sent him a look of affectionate exasperation. 'Oh, Ken, why can't you be more open? You persist in keeping secrets long after the need for them has gone. Is there anything else I ought to know?'

He took a deep breath.

'Well?'

'Only that . . . in addition to being an extremely good dancer, my mother also makes the best desserts going . . . and some have even been known to refer to her as The Hot Pudding Queen.'

'Some?' Her eyes were teasing.

'All right then, just one. Me. The Hot Pudding Queen isn't my girlfriend, Lisa . . . I just wanted to clear that up.'

She bit back a smile of delight. The Hot Pudding Queen wasn't his girl-friend. And if she had been mistaken about that, then maybe she'd been mistaken about other things too.

Maybe it was time to leave things to fate and take a few risks, and if, in the end, she and Ken weren't meant to be together, she'd still have beautiful memories to look back on, and the knowledge that she'd had the courage to take a chance.

'I expect you think I tend to jump to conclusions,' she whispered, as Daisy appeared with their order.

'Just a bit.' He gave a wry smile. 'You and I need to have a long talk and get a few things sorted out.'

'How about this lunchtime?' she said, once Daisy had gone again. 'You don't have to be at the class until two, so we could go back to my flat and talk while we eat. I won't be able to cook, of course, but I'd be happy to buy in.'

She waited, her heart pounding. That had been really forward! Oh, why couldn't she think before she spoke instead of jumping straight in?

'Look, forget I said that,' she added hastily. 'You've probably got other arrangements. Don't worry. We'll do it some other time.'

He reached across the table and took her hand. 'I've promised to have lunch with Simone today,' he said gently, 'but I'm free later on tonight, so why don't we have that take-away then?'

So he'd found another distraction already — and the sad thing was that if she hadn't been so determined to keep him at bay, the situation may never have arisen.

'You're on.' She picked up her spoon. 'How are things working out with Simone, by the way? You haven't told me much about her.'

Ken was studying his ice cream. 'What's to tell?' he asked. 'She's good at her job, and the students all like her.'

But is she pretty? Lisa wanted to scream out. And do you fancy her more than you do me?

Ken studied her with a curious smile. 'From your expression, that obviously isn't enough. What else do you want to know?'

'I was just wondering if she's

anything like me,' she said, slanting him a glance from under her lashes. 'We women like to know these things.'

He was trying not to laugh. She could see the gleam of suppressed merriment dancing in his eyes.

'No, she's not really like you. But you needn't worry, she's doing an excellent job.'

'Maybe I should come and meet her. It seems strange leaving my classes in the hands of someone I've never met.'

'I wouldn't do that. It might seem as though you don't trust her. Take my word for it, she's doing OK.'

Lisa knew when she was being fobbed off, and she also knew that unless she was prepared to put up a fight, Simone could easily snatch Ken from under her nose.

'In which case, why don't you and I have that talk tonight?' she said softly.

He smiled. 'I'll be round as soon as I can.'

* * *

Lisa was still thinking about Simone long after Ken had gone on his way, and continued to do so for the next couple of hours. Was she small and bouncy with a pert line in chat, or was she an experienced woman of the world? And how did Ken act around her? Was there the same caustic banter as he shared with her, or did they exchange deep, soulful looks with hardly a word passing between them?

Lisa had to know — and quickly. How could she possibly compete with the opposition when she had no idea of what she was up against?

It took two minutes to order a taxi and another fifteen for it to arrive, but by three o'clock, Lisa was hauling herself across the foyer of the Cliff Hotel, prepared to answer her own questions.

She'd arrived mid-way through the lesson. The door leading to the ball-room was open, but a drape screened the dancers from prying eyes and effectively sectioned the whole area off.

Gently and unobtrusively, she pulled back an edge of the curtain and focussed her gaze on the stage. No wonder her students couldn't get enough of Ken. With his dark good looks and a frame that would be the envy of any athlete, the mere sight of him was sufficient to set hearts hammering and pulses racing — and nobody's more strongly than Lisa's.

But it was the small figure to his left that captured her interest. The woman's head mike and confident manner marked her out as the teacher, but her white hair and lined face placed her at somewhere between sixty and seventy years old.

With a sigh of pure happiness, Lisa let the curtain fall. She'd wait until the end of the lesson and then go in and introduce herself. Simone surely wouldn't mind that?

Lisa repositioned her crutches, then made her way back to the reception area.

'Nice to see you back, Miss,' the

doorman said. 'Even if it's not for long.'

Lisa went cold. 'What do you mean?'

'Only two weeks before the ballroom closes.'

His face fell when he saw her stunned expression.

'I'm sorry, I thought you knew. The place is set to become a conference suite. Mr Huntley finally confirmed it at yesterday's staff meeting. The builders move in the week after next.'

For a moment, Lisa didn't believe she'd heard him correctly.

'So soon?' she whispered. 'But I thought . . .'

'That it would be around for ever? I think most of us here did too. But apparently conference facilities are far more lucrative than big old-fashioned ballrooms, so this one's for the chop.'

She couldn't answer. This was the last thing she'd been expecting to hear and it was all too much to take in. How could Ken do this to her? After all he'd promised? After all he'd said?

'Excuse me, I think I left something

in the taxi,' she managed at last and turned away.

Once outside, it was all Lisa could do not to dissolve into tears. What a fool she'd been to place her trust in Ken. Taking her out that morning had been nothing more than a calculated ploy on his part to keep boredom at bay. No doubt there'd have been several more such visits over the coming weeks, all designed to keep her well away from the hotel.

And it would have worked, too, if the green-eyed monster hadn't reared its ugly head and sent her to check out Simone.

How could she have been so foolish? She should have realised that a man so set on modernisation and progress wasn't going to place her needs top of his list. He'd wanted her out from the beginning and in order to throw her off guard, had told her everything she'd wanted to hear — and the sad truth of the matter was, he'd very nearly succeeded.

Life Without Ken

Lisa hardly remembered the journey back to her flat. All she was aware of was the ache in her heart. Ken had proved to be no different from her father — buoying her up with soft words and sweet promises, only to leave her to fall back to earth with a thud.

But there was no way she was going to take issue with him and let him discover what she'd found out. She still had her pride, and intended to summon up every last remnant, to emerge from the situation with dignity and decorum. Ken would never know how much he meant to her, and once he was out of her life for good, she might find it possible to forget.

When he turned up that evening, Lisa led him into the living-room and invited him to sit down.

He complied with a grin. 'This is

very formal. When I said we needed to talk, it wasn't exactly a business meeting I had in mind.'

She manoeuvred herself on to the settee and propped her crutches neatly at her side.

'I know, and that's what concerns me.'

'Really? What's on your mind?'

'There's not much to tell,' she said, keeping her voice flat and dispassionate. 'I've been grateful for your help these last few days, and I don't know how I'd have coped without you.'

'I sense a but,' he murmured, the teasing light fading from his eyes.

'But now I'm managing the crutches and able to get around, I think it's best that the visits stop.'

He looked at her oddly. 'So what's brought this on? This morning you seemed quite happy with the way things were going, and now suddenly you don't want me around.'

'What you're doing — coming here each day to see to the kittens, taking me out in your car — it's putting the relationship on a personal footing, and frankly I'm not comfortable with that.'

'I see.' He remained thoughtful. 'Excuse me if I'm being a bit slow at taking this in, but I really didn't see it coming.'

'The fact is, Ken . . . ' Her voice was unsteady, but her determination resolute. 'I can never feel anything for you except as a friend — '

'And you don't want me to embarrass myself by pushing for more?'

She nodded miserably.

'And what I also wanted to tell you,' she blurted out in an unhappy rush, 'is that I've decided to close my business down and return to my home town to live. So we won't be coming into contact with each other for very much longer.'

For a long moment she thought he wasn't going to answer, then he abruptly got to his feet.

'I can't pretend this hasn't come as a shock,' he said quietly, 'but if it's true, then I've obviously read the signs all wrong.'

'Of course it's true. I'm not in the habit of telling lies.'

He crouched beside her. 'If this has anything to do with the way I misled you over my mother . . . ' He tipped her chin up so she had to meet his eyes. 'I promise you, Lisa, it's not something I'm proud of or would choose to do again. Deception isn't part of my nature.'

Lisa jerked her head aside, feeling physically sick. How could he say that? After what he'd done to her business, the incident with his mother paled into insignificance.

'There's no point in going into all the whys and wherefores,' she said, refusing to meet his eyes. 'The fact of the matter is, I don't feel anything for you, and want all contact between us to end. I owe my students the courtesy of a couple of weeks' notice, so I'd like the classes to finish according to our original agreement — two weeks from today.'

He stood up. 'In that case, there's nothing more to be said.' He moved towards the door. 'Or is there?'

'No,' she whispered, staring blankly ahead. 'I really don't think there is.'

Her gaze drifted involuntarily towards him and her stomach clenched with unexpected regret as she met his bewildered stare.

'Please, Ken, just go. This is awkward enough as it is, without you prolonging it.'

She held herself together until she heard the final click of the door, then buried her face in a cushion and sobbed.

When she finally raised her head and dried her eyes, Ken had been gone for the best part of an hour. In that time, she'd contemplated going after him to tell him she hadn't meant what she'd said . . . that her life would be bleak and empty without him.

But deep in her heart she knew it wouldn't solve a thing. What she needed to do now was get on with her life, and get as far away from Ken Huntley as possible.

There was only one flaw in that argument . . .

* * *

When she picked up the phone the next morning, it was with the intention of leaving a message at Reception, but before she'd had chance to collect her thoughts, the receptionist put her through to Ken.

Her hand trembled on the receiver.

'Ken, it's Lisa,' she said. 'It's about my sound system and CDs. I'd like to collect them straight after the last class has ended. Could you arrange to have it all waiting for me?'

'Don't you owe it to your students to actually be at the class? Bowing out without any explanation's a little cowardly, don't you think?'

The harshness of his tone made her wince. But he was right, she thought bleakly. The least she could do was close the class herself and thank everyone for their loyal support.

'Yes, you're right,' she said at last. 'I'll arrive sometime during the last half hour, if you could incorporate that into your schedule.'

Her hand was shaking when she hung up the receiver. It wasn't going to be easy, going back and seeing him again — but she had no choice.

Despite Lisa having plenty to occupy her physically over the next two weeks, mentally it was a different story. When she wasn't dreaming of Ken, she was imagining his car pulling up outside her flat, or expecting him to be at the other end of the phone every time it rang. He might be out of her life, but in her mind he featured as prominently as ever.

The truth of the matter was, she'd never get over him, and things would only start to get better when she'd put enough distance between them to ensure their paths would never cross again.

* ★ *

Her ordeal was almost over, Lisa told herself, as she hobbled through the entrance of the hotel. She'd forced her breathing to normal, ready to confront him, when she realised — there was nobody waiting to greet her!

But then, she reasoned, why should there be? Ken was hardly likely to leave the dancers without any music while he waited in the foyer for her.

Not a sound came from behind the curtain, and when Lisa tentatively tugged it aside, her gaze fell on an empty room.

No Ken. No Simone. No dancers; just a dimly-lit shell of a ballroom. Where were the crystal chandeliers? The luxurious red drapes? The sparkling mirrors, the spotlights, the stage? Devoid of its glitzy trappings the room looked surprisingly age-worn — drab, tired and out-dated.

So Ken had begun ripping it apart already. He couldn't even be trusted to allow her one final meeting with her students!

But as quickly as it arose, her indignation fell away, to be replaced by relief. He'd also spared her the ordeal of having to explain why the classes were closing, and dissolving into tears in the middle of her speech.

She moved farther into the room. Stripped of its cosmetic enhancements, the ballroom seemed huge and daunting, and the task of refurbishing it phenomenal. Even if Ken had been persuaded to retain it, there was no guarantee that anyone except Lisa would have had any use for it.

He'd been right all along. This was the twenty-first century, not the Edwardian era, and if the hotel was to prosper, it needed to ditch its outmoded image and move into the here and now.

Wearily, Lisa sank into a chair, her body sagging with regret. She'd felt angry and upset that Ken hadn't understood the ballroom's importance to her, and she'd behaved as if she were the only one who mattered. But if he'd been stubborn and selfish, then so had she. Unforgivably and unreasonably so.

He'd told her often enough that her classes couldn't figure in his plans, and she'd obstinately refused to accept it. She'd placed him in an impossible position. *I can't love you unless you give me the ballroom* had been her message, and if he couldn't, then it was goodbye for ever.

The sad thing was, she realised, in the end, Ken had mattered far more to her than the ballroom — but she'd been too self-centred to see it. She'd lost both her business and Ken, and she had only herself to blame.

'Hello, Lisa,' a gentle voice spoke. 'Glad you could make it.'

She jerked her head round. 'Ken . . .'

As he came towards her, the soft lamplight illuminating the uncertainty on his face, it was all she could do not to hurl herself into his arms. But she'd sacrificed that right when she'd sent him away, and now there was no going back.

'Ken . . . ' she repeated, her voice a whisper. 'I'm so very sorry.'

He came closer. 'For what?' he asked softly. 'For not caring? Or for letting me believe that you did?'

Tears blurred her vision.

'I loved you, Lisa,' he said with a heart-rending sadness. 'You must have realised that.'

The ache inside her grew. He'd said loved, not love — anything they'd had was in the past.

'And the strange thing is, up until two weeks ago I'd begun to believe you might feel something for me too. Then suddenly you didn't want to know me.'

Lisa didn't answer. She couldn't. If only they could turn back the clock and start again, the outcome could have been so very different.

He reached out to take her shoulders. 'Why, Lisa? What did I do to make you change towards me?'

His voice was so thick and husky it

was barely recognisable, and as she gazed back at his anguished expression, she knew that even if it meant sacrificing every shred of pride, she couldn't go on lying to him.

'I was angry,' she began, her heart beating so loudly that she thought Ken must surely hear it too. 'I came to the ballroom after you'd asked me not to, and found out you were planning on closing it permanently.'

He regarded her silently, his dark eyes unreadable.

'I didn't stay. I couldn't, but by that evening I'd managed to convince myself that if I couldn't trust you in business, then I couldn't trust you in anything, and that there was no point in us continuing to meet.'

'And now?'

'The hotel is your living . . . and in order to bring it into the twenty-first century, the ballroom has to go. I accept that now, and love you too much to let it come between us.' Her voice was shaking. 'I don't care if I never find another venue to equal it. I'll operate from a string of church halls if I have to . . . if it means there's a chance of us being together.'

'That's an extremely generous offer, but totally unnecessary.'

Hope died. 'You don't want us to be together?' she whispered.

He cupped her face in his hands. 'There's nothing I want more,' he murmured, his fingers gently caressing her cheeks. 'But remember, I said I'd never ask you to leave the ballroom until you'd been offered a suitable replacement, and I've no intention of going back on that.'

She gave a humourless laugh. 'I remember that, but I'd already checked out endless places, long before I met you, and I knew you couldn't keep that promise. I used the knowledge to push you into a corner, Ken, and I can't blame you for backing out.'

'If my backing out had been as callous as you imagined, then you had every right to feel angry and let down.'

She lifted her lashes to search his expression for sincerity. 'We both know you had no choice. You needed me out and there was nowhere for me to go. Between us we must have exhausted every last possibility.'

He placed a finger on her lips. 'Except for one.'

She felt her stomach quiver.

'The old theatre. I've transferred the fixtures and fittings over there from the ballroom and given the place a total revamp. Simone and my mother are there now with your students, waiting for you to join them. It's all yours, Lisa, converted with love, as my wedding present to you.'

It took a moment for his words to sink in.

'Wedding present?' she whispered. 'You — want to marry me?'

His voice was hoarse. 'Desperately. I'd planned to ask you two weeks ago, the night I came to your flat. I was so sure you'd accept that I'd already started work on the theatre and was planning to surprise you.'

Tears welled in her eyes. 'I don't know what to say.'

He caught her hands and lifted them to his lips. 'You could try 'yes'.'

'Oh, yes,' she whispered. 'I can't think of anything I'd like more.'

The next instant his arms were around her, and he was kissing her as if he never intended to let her go. Lisa's heart sang. It was all right — everything was going to be all right.

Yet . . .

'So why the lunch date with Simone?' she murmured.

His lips brushed her temple. 'The lunch was a thank you for letting me pick her brains. With her advice and my mother's, I managed to come up with a conversion plan that could be carried out in a very short time.'

'Oh Ken — and you still carried on, even after I'd sent you away . . . ' Her voice broke.

'Not immediately,' he admitted, 'but when I heard you'd been here that day, it dawned on me what had happened, so I decided to press ahead. I decided to give you some time to cool down and then try talking to you again. It was a risk, but one worth taking. And besides . . . '

'What?'

His mouth quirked. 'I figured you were hardly likely to go out clubbing and meet someone else, with that plaster cast on your leg.'

Before she could answer, he'd swept her up into his arms and was carrying her towards the door.

'Where are you taking me?' she demanded on a whoop of laughter.

'First stop the theatre,' he said, ignoring her protests. 'You might have got out of making one announcement, but you're not ducking out of this one. I want everyone to hear about our engagement and to know you'll be coming back.'

'And then?'

He nodded towards the bar. 'And then we'll crack open a bottle of champagne. I've got my two favourite females back into my life, and I don't intend to let that pass without a celebration.'

'Two? Is there something else you haven't told me?'

'Scaredy-Cat's back.'

Ken bent his head to hers again and they exchanged a kiss — a kiss of exquisite sweetness, filled with all the love and passion and promise their hearts could hold.

THE END

We do hope that you have enjoyed reading this large print book.

Did you know that all of our titles are available for purchase?

We publish a wide range of high quality large print books including:
Romances, Mysteries, Classics
General Fiction
Non Fiction and Westerns

Special interest titles available in large print are:
The Little Oxford Dictionary
Music Book, Song Book
Hymn Book, Service Book

Also available from us courtesy of Oxford University Press:
Young Readers' Dictionary
(large print edition)
Young Readers' Thesaurus
(large print edition)

For further information or a free brochure, please contact us at:
Ulverscroft Large Print Books Ltd.,
The Green, Bradgate Road, Anstey,
Leicester, LE7 7FU, England.
Tel: (00 44) **0116 236 4325**
Fax: (00 44) **0116 234 0205**

Other titles in the
Linford Romance Library:

REBECCA'S REVENGE

Valerie Holmes

Rebecca Hind's life is thrown into turmoil when her brother mysteriously disappears and she cannot keep up rent payments for their humble cottage. Help is offered by Mr Paignton of Gorebeck Lodge, although Rebecca is reluctant to leave with him and his mysterious companion. However, faced with little choice and determined to survive, Rebecca takes the offered position at the Lodge — and enters a strange world where she finds hate and love living side by side . . .

HIDDEN PLACES

Chrissie Loveday

Young widow Lauren and her son Scott have emigrated to New Zealand, where they inherit an unusual home set in a thermal park. Lauren keeps the park running smoothly for tourists, but struggles with the huge task. Desperate for help, her advertisement for assistance is answered by hunky Travis, and she believes her problems are solved. But there are major troubles ahead and important decisions to be made. Both love and deception will play a part in her dramatic new life.